The Smoke

Tales from a Revolution: New-York

Also by Lars D. H. Hedbor,
available from Brief Candle Press:

The Prize: Tales From a Revolution - Vermont
The Light: Tales From a Revolution - New-Jersey
The Declaration: Tales From a Revolution - South-Carolina
The Break: Tales From a Revolution - Nova-Scotia
The Wind: Tales From a Revolution - West-Florida
The Darkness: Tales From a Revolution - Maine
The Path: Tales From a Revolution - Rhode-Island
The Freedman: Tales From a Revolution - North-Carolina
The Tree: Tales From a Revolution - New-Hampshire

The Smoke

Lars D. H. Hedbor

Brief Candle
Press

Cover and book design: Brief Candle Press
Cover image based on "Indian Sunset: Deer by a Lake," Albert Bierstadt.
Map reproductions courtesy of the Library of Congress, Geography and Map Division.
Fonts: Allegheney, Doves Type and IM FELL English.

Third Printing

First Brief Candle Press edition published 2014
www.briefcandlepress.com

ISBN: 978-0-9894410-4-9

Dedication

To Jenn,
without whom
none of this would be possible

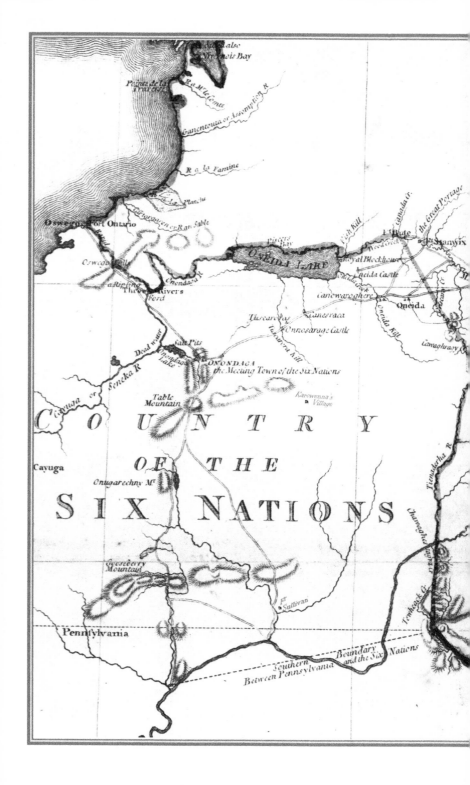

Chapter I

Tanarou awoke to the smell of smoke. He sat upright from his pallet, drawing the skin around his shoulders as he looked about him to locate its source. The morning sunlight filtered through the riotously-colored leaves of autumn, casting a pattern of ever-changing shadow across the floor of the forest around his sleeping place.

Nearby, he saw his companion Ginawo stirring in his sleep, but he knew that the younger man would be slower to wake than he was, with his senses fully sharpened by the experience of combat. Standing, Tanarou moved silently into the woods toward the source of the acrid scent, seeking its cause.

As he crested a rise tangled with low-hanging cedars he spotted the small campfire, and heard the guttural speech of three men who lounged about it. Freezing, he studied them. They did not wear the blood-colored jackets that marked warriors of the "British" tribe distinctly from those of the "Colonial" tribe.

Their clothing was worn and dirty by Tanarou's standards, made of the material that looked like skins, but was composed of many individual strands, in a variety of shades, ranging from the pale brown of dried grass to the black of a doe's eye.

Their words were in English, though Tanarou's grasp of that language was not firm enough for him to make out more than a handful of words. He did hear the word "Indian" from one, who wore a rough jacket of poorly-cured deerskin and a hat bearing a bright blue ribbon Tanarou knew somehow signified his rank.

One of the deerskin man's companions responded with a long comment, from which Tanarou could only recognize the words "scalp" and "Mohawk," which Tanarou knew was the word that these pale men used for some of his brothers.

The topic of their conversation was deeply interesting to him, so he knew that Ginawo's hare ears should be the ones to listen in on it. His companion's youth might be a hindrance in early-morning alertness, but like young men of all times and places, Ginawo had embraced and absorbed the novelty of the ever-increasing presence and contact with these new men with greater enthusiasm than the men of Tanarou's generation had.

As a result, Ginawo understood much of the English that most of these men spoke amongst themselves, as well as some of the French that others spoke. To Tanarou, none of these tongues had the fluid beauty of the words taught to his own people in the days before the stories were told, the true words of the People.

Regardless of the aesthetic merits of the language these interlopers used, Tanarou needed to understand better what they spoke about, so he slipped back over the ridge, relaxing as he was safe from the view of the men lazing about the smoky fire that had betrayed their presence to all creatures for a great many strides downwind.

Returning to where Ginawo still slumbered, he bent beside the younger man, grunting softly in his ear, "Wake, you who would mimic the wintering bear. It is not yet time for your long sleep, and there is work I need of you."

Ginawo opened one eye and looked at Tanarou, saying in

a whisper that matched Tanarou's low volume, "You are not the straight-limbed maiden I hoped to find stepping out of my night thoughts. What is it that you need of me, respected elder?" His tone as he said these last words failed to reflect the honor due to Tanarou, and earned him a quiet, but not too hard, cuff on the ear.

"There is a group of the pale men whose fire should have awakened you long before I returned, and I need you to tell me what they are saying to one another and all who would care to listen."

Ginawo opened his other eye and sniffed the air, nodding to Tanarou. "You are right, as usual, revered elder. I have erred in not awakening sooner." Rising to his feet, the younger man stood slightly taller than Tanarou, a fact that the old warrior resented but refused to acknowledge that he resented. Narrowing his eyes and pointing with his chin, Ginawo continued, "They lie in that direction?"

Tanarou nodded in reply and led the way. Neither man made any sound as they stepped through the confusion of tangled fallen branches and the carpet of fresh leaves that laid on the forest floor. Both wore the skins of the bear in whose brotherhood they were joined, scraped clean and made supple by the long, patient application of the thick, pungent grease of the same animals.

Warm and flexible, the more important feature of these clothes at the moment was that they enabled the men to blend in invisibly with the forest around them. Neither had a firearm, and they knew that in a conflict with the pale men, they would be overcome in a moment—so they kept themselves invisible to the blind eyes of the interlopers, and inaudible to their deaf ears.

Stopping as the smell of the campfire nearly brought a sneeze to his nose, Tanarou motioned for Ginawo to follow slowly now as they came within hearing of the Colonial men's speech. The two stopped behind the boles of great maples, each large enough that even if the other men had thought to look in their direction, there would be nothing that they could spot, even if they could truly see.

From this vantage, they listened, Tanarou only picking up an odd word now and again, and Ginawo carefully marking everything he could say. The younger man's special gift was in being able to repeat stories he heard, whether they were the stories of the Elders, spoken in the speech of the People, or the words of such as these three men, with their broken-sounding languages. He would later be able to recite what he heard, and then tell Tanarou—or others—everything that he understood of it.

Tanarou could hear laughter and a lot of what sounded like relatively light-hearted banter, though it was difficult to discern exactly what the mood of the speech he heard was, so different was it to his ear. The few words he could make out sounded warlike, in contradiction to the tone, and he looked forward to Ginawo's report of the details.

As they sat listening, they could hear the men stand and begin to clean up their encampment, to the extent that they could be bothered. The hiss of water poured over the campfire, accompanied by a pale drift of dying-ember smoke and the warm smell of steam, told Tanarou that it was time for he and his companion to return to the place where they had spent the night themselves, so that they could discuss what Ginawo had heard.

Motioning silently to Ginawo, Tanarou rose to a crouch and made his way down the slope and back toward their camp. After a noment, Ginawo rose to follow him, and Tanarou heard the crack of a branch snapping beneath the younger man's moccasined foot, as he incautiously stepped away from his tree.

Ginawo and Tanarou both froze, and the talk from the men on the other side fell silent, as all five men fought panic and fear of what would happen next. Tanarou could hear the Colonials trying to be quiet as they ranged out from their campsite in search of the source of the sound that they'd heard. He discerned that they were heading in the wrong direction, though, and he motioned to Ginawo to follow him in the opposite direction.

He did not express recriminations to the younger man for his carelessness—there would be time enough for that later—but in his heart, Tanarou raged at Ginawo's oafishness. Clever he might be, but if he got himself or both men killed, all his recitations and translations would be of less use than antlers to a wolf.

Now, at least, however, Ginawo was being fully mindful of his footfalls, and Tanarou himself had to glance back from time to time to assure himself that the younger man followed him yet. The Colonials had started shouting to each other as they fruitlessly scouted over the hillside, and he could make out enough to recognize that they were convincing themselves that it had been something other than a human footstep that they had heard.

Tanarou led Ginawo further away from their encounter with the pale men, speeding up as the need for utter silence fell away with distance. Finally, he signaled a halt, and waited for Ginawo to join him for a conference.

As Ginawo approached, he lowered his shoulders and presented Tanarou his ear for the painful cuff he had earned, and accepted it without flinching or crying out. "I was careless and foolish, honored elder, and I am deeply grateful that my error did not cost us more dearly."

"Well you should be filled with sorrow, Ginawo, who stumbles through the woods like a currant-drunk turkey. If those pale men had not been as stupid as newly-born squirrels, we would be their captives or worse now."

"I know this, respected elder, and I only hope that the knowledge I have carried away from our meeting with them will be worth the danger I then brought to us."

"What have you learned, drunken turkey?"

Ginawo favored the older man with a crooked smile. "If you will refrain from sharing that name with the others ever, I will gladly tell you what the Colonial warriors were speaking of."

Tanarou feigned giving the matter some serious consideration, and then nodded solemnly. "I will not tell Jiwaneh that you have more in common with an autumn turkey than with a great warrior, if you will now share with me what those men spoke of."

Ginawo flushed at the mention of his favorite girl's name, but he took a deep breath and nodded before he began to speak.

"They are a scouting party, and a much larger force follows them two days back."

"What is their purpose in coming to this place?"

"They did not speak of this, but they did say that they would be looking for settlements of the People to report back to their chief."

Tanarou's brow furrowed deeply at this news. "They cannot be looking for us in order to make gifts to us," he muttered, mostly to himself.

Since the British and the Colonials had begun warring

several summers before, Tanarou and many of the other elders of both tribe and clan had been torn as to what the role of the People ought to be in this new struggle.

First to speak at the conclave where they gathered to talk the question over had been Hotoke, who reported, "We have already heard that our clan-brothers in the other tribes of the Haudenosaunee have been participating in attacks on the Colonials, and have destroyed several of their villages and taken trophies of their victories."

He gestured to the east and continued, "I have spoken with Oskanondonha, who would have us fight alongside the Colonials and in opposition to our own clan-brothers. Already he has set brother against brother, tribe against tribe. This is no way for the People to treat one another."

The elder Nakawe had been unequivocal. "We should learn which side in this war can most benefit the People. We have always been able to enjoy the ruin of these pale men when they contest with one another."

He gestured about the lodge at the gathered elders, urging their agreement with his hands and nods of his head. "Perhaps this time, they will even grow so small from grinding upon each other like rocks in a stream that we can pluck them out and toss them back into the ocean."

Many had murmured their agreement, but old Nitchawake had stood, commanding silence with his presence. Slowly, the discussions around the lodge had slid to a halt until all in the circle looked at him and waited for his comments.

"Many wars have I seen, between brothers in the People, between the People and these men, and amongst these men themselves. I have seen peoples ground down as you say. Our tribe is one such, and we now live on this land because my father and his brothers made the same mistake you are making."

He surveyed the room, opening his arms to encompass the world outside of the lodge. As did all in the circle, Tanarou attended him closely, and not only because of his age. His skin and hair were tinted darkly with the costly root of their former homeland, giving him a dark visage that all present instinctively associated with strength and experience.

"My father fought in the war for the warm skies, and he was among the dead there. My mother told me many times of the welcoming home of the People by our brothers in the Haudenosaunee Confederation."

His arms dropped as he settled into his tale. "We were forced out of lands warmer and more genial than this place, where we had been masters of our own fate. The other tribes of the Confederation make the People feel welcome here, but in games at the clan gatherings as I grew up, I sometimes heard my brothers and myself taunted for our need to carry more fur in winter, and for the ways of our mothers."

He shook his head. "My aunts and uncles did not come here because they wished to speak with others whose tongues were familiar to them. They came here because an entire generation of warriors was laid low in battle with these pale men, the same men whom you so lightly assume can be depended upon to grind themselves away in dissipation against their own brothers."

Sitting, he concluded, "It may be that we will need to choose a tribe of the pale men to call our brothers in war as they fight each other. But we must do so like the hare, who runs swiftly because knows that he is easy to catch, and not like the porcupine, who tastes just as good, but stands to fight because he believes himself to be invincible."

A long silence followed Nitchiwake's speech, and in the quiet, the even older Karowenna spoke up from her place of honor on a mat at the end of the circle furthest from the entrance to the lodge. "Nitchiwake is right—but we are neither hare nor porcupine. We are not helpless, nor are we foolish."

Her eyes narrowed in the deep and complex folds of her face, and she continued, "We are like the fox, wise enough to see trouble when it is coming, and swift enough to flee, should it prove to be more than our teeth can hold."

She paused for a long moment, so long that Tanarou even thought that she might have fallen asleep. He nearly started when she said, suddenly, "Neither side of this war has treated us fairly. Both the blood-jackets and the farm-builders will take what they need, without regard for the People. Indeed, they do not see us as people at all, but rather merely as a hindrance to their own plans."

She, too, shook her head in frustration. "None of them can be trusted to keep their word; none can be left unwatched with something that is ours that they might want. We should take no side today, but rather regard all of them as enemies not yet at war with us."

There had been much more conversation in the lodge, lasting late into the night, but ultimately, the elders as a group had come to the same conclusion, and so things stood as Tanarou considered what to make of the information that Ginawo had reported to him.

Tanarou asked the younger man, "Did they say specifically

that they were looking for the People, or for some of our brother tribes? I heard them speak of the Mohawk before I came and disturbed your sleep."

"I did not hear them speak of any tribe. They only said that they needed to look for all of the villages in the area."

The younger man scowled and added, "I did not like the way that they laughed when they said that they hoped to find our villages without alerting us. Should we summon the warriors?"

Tanarou frowned. "To what end?"

"We can stop the scouts from finding our homes!"

"Did they say how large the force is that is following them? I have little doubt that if we stopped them, they would send out more scouts, and in larger numbers." The older man shook his head. "No, we must simply warn the People and hope that they can escape whatever mischief these pale men have in their minds for us. The fox does not attack the wolf, Ginawo, but instead stays out of his way when he comes to visit."

Ginawo scowled even more deeply, but kept his thoughts to himself.

Tanarou rose and listened carefully for a moment, then said, "Come, let us return to where we slept, so that we can conceal our presence there, should they happen to stumble across it."

Chapter 2

Sergeant John Howe wearily joined his men as they finished cleaning up the last traces of the night's encampment. William and Joseph, his two privates, exchanged amused glances as they packed up their kit and tossed leaves and fallen branches over the site of their fire to conceal the fact that they'd been there.

As he worked, William asked conversationally, "Do you figure that it were an animal, then, Sergeant?"

Howe sighed wearily. "I don't know, William. It sounded like a branch breaking under the weight of a man, but we never did see any hint of anyone in the woods." He scowled up at the ridgeline where he'd thought he'd heard the tell-tale sign that they were not alone in the forest.

"Of course, with those devils, who could even tell? I've heard stories that they scarcely even touch the ground as they go, so it's no wonder that they leave no tracks that a normal man could follow. I can track most any creature on four legs or two, but they seem able to leave no mark, even when they've left no doubt that they've been there."

Joseph looked up, a sad, distant look in his eye. "They left nothing but ashes at my neighbor's place in Pennsylvania. Naught even fit to bury left of them."

He looked sharply at Howe. "Nor any tracks any of us could see, either. They are devils, when they set their minds to it."

After pondering for a few moments, he added, "Some of them can be downright helpful, but these Mohawks and Iroquois are just set on murder and destruction, it seems. Is it true that we're going to give them back some of their own?"

Howe shook his head and pursed his lips. "Nay, I cannot say what is on the general's mind exactly. He has his orders from General Washington himself, though, and authorization right from the Congress, so whatever they've told him to do, it's all the way from the top."

William interjected, "Well, whatever it is, I hope we can get on with it soon. Weather's not getting any warmer, and them dandies in Congress can't seem to get us any warm clothes to wear out here."

"Nice morning today, though, particularly since we're warmed up from beating through the woods," Howe rejoined, and all three men laughed. Slinging their sacks onto their shoulders, the two privates looked expectantly to Howe, who glanced at the sun rising through the leaves over his right shoulder and started his little squad marching northward.

As they picked their way through the undergrowth, Joseph started in again on a constant complaint. "Sergeant, will we be getting some more supplies in a few days, when we report in? My belly still feels empty, even though I know that we just ate."

Howe shook his head, frustrated. "Joseph, you'd still be peckish even after you finished off an entire steer. I think that your legs must be hollow, because there's no other reason that you don't outweigh any three other men in the squad, the way you eat."

"Aw, come on, sergeant! I don't eat any more than is my share."

"...plus whatever the rest of us leave on our plates," intoned William quietly.

Joseph answered plaintively, "Well, would you have me just let it go to waste?"

The two privates bickered on, mostly in good spirits, as the little group continued to make its way through the forest until it was full well time to do something about Joseph's growling belly. Howe said, "Stop here, men, and let's have a small, quick fire for some tea and hardtack, all right?"

Joseph was very efficient about getting the fire going, busily gathering dry kindling from the undergrowth, and within a few minutes, a fire crackled within the circle of rocks he had assembled in the small clearing Howe had selected for their resting point.

William was just as fast to set up the pot over the fire and scraped tea into the pot from the block he produced out of his sack. Shortly, all three were slurping the last drops of tea from around the dregs in their battered tin cups and gnawing at their hardtack.

They stomped out the embers and covered them with dirt before re-arraying the natural detritus of the woods about the spot. Once Howe declared himself satisfied that their presence would not be betrayed by any remnants of their fire, they again shouldered their packs and continued into the forest.

The sunlight of the morning had given way to sullen grey clouds by the time they stopped for lunch, and not long after they began marching northward again, the first drops of cold rain were spattering through the orange and yellow leaves of the autumn trees. The three men raised their collars, and the tricorn design of their hats kept the worst of the drips from the branches overhead off of their necks.

"How long do you reckon before this turns to snow?" Joseph's tone was just short of a whine, and William grinned at Howe's growl in response.

"Now that we've filled your belly, must we listen to your complaints about the Congress' management of the weather for the next ten miles?"

Joseph replied, aggrieved, "I wasn't complaining, only but wondering. After all, I expect that it starts snowing sooner here in New York than it does in Pennsylvania."

"You've naught to worry about, Joseph," Howe replied. "I misdoubt that even Congress will expect us to fight once the snows in these parts get going."

William spoke up now, interjecting, "I've heard tell that the snow here can get to be deep enough that a man could pick apples without a ladder, if he could but stay upright in the stuff." After a moment's thought, he added, "Or if there were any apples yet to pick by the time the snow became that deep."

"Indeed, William, when last I traveled here, I heard much the same, but if we find ourselves still in these reaches of the country by that time, we'll likely all get the chance to learn how to use snow-shoes. Our opponents here are known to be expert users of these things, and it will not avail us at all to say that we cannot meet them in battle because there is snow on the ground."

Joseph replied, animatedly, "I have heard of these things, that they permit a man to walk on snow just as if he were floating over the top!"

"'Tis not so easy as that, Joseph," Howe said. "I have spoken with men who have used them, and they say that it is hard work—not so hard as walking in snow without them, but still, a fit man can only go perhaps half so far in a day with them than he could on dry ground, and he will rest well that night."

"Speaking of rest...," Joseph began, hopefully, but Howe silenced him with a glare.

"The village we're to scout out is twenty miles ahead yet, and then we return to the main force to share what intelligence we have gathered. We'll not succeed in this if we don't keep up a decent pace."

"Yes, sir," said Joseph, his shoulders slumping. However, his pace never slackened, and the group made good time through the now-sodden woods.

With the heavy clouds overhead still providing a steady rain, it grew too dark for safe travel much earlier than it had the previous evening, and Howe soon enough ordered the men to stop and set up camp for the night.

No one in the group was an experienced woodsman—William had been a blacksmith's apprentice prior to his enlistment in the militia, Joseph a farmer, and Howe had been a brewer.

However, they had learned quickly enough how to fashion the canvas they carried into a rude shelter, and with a few saplings and some hempen twine, they soon had a serviceable lean-to tent that they could sleep under.

As he laid the fire, Joseph swore under his breath. "This kindling is so wet, it's going to take a long blow indeed to make a decent fire with it."

When his companions failed to express their sympathy, busy with their own tasks around the campsite, he shook his head and went back to setting the thinnest cedar branches he'd collected into a careful pile over the bark and somewhat dry leaves he'd already formed into a loose circle in the fire pit.

Sighing again, he pulled a cord of jute twine from his tinder box and carefully unraveled it into a loose, dry form, which he then set into the center of the fire pit. Crumpling up charcloth around that, he then pulled out the flint and his knife, and began scraping sparks into the jute.

"Ha!" He gave a quiet exclamation of victory as the jute caught light, and bent hurriedly to give it breath and encourage it into a full fire. Soon enough, the charcloth had lit up the leaves and bark, and the first from the kindling-wood starting to burn let him sit back on his heels as he carefully laid larger sticks and wood across the small fire and built it into a warm, cheerful presence in the center of the campsite.

"Fire's ready," he called to William, who had already unpacked his cooking kit, and was pouring the water Howe had fetched back from the nearby stream into his cook pot.

"Thanks, Joseph. See? It wasn't so hard as you thought it'd be."

Joseph grunted noncommittally, and Howe smiled from inside the lean-to, where he was unfolding the waxcloth upon which they would sleep—hopefully, dry.

William fed some dried beef into the pot that he'd set over the fire, and then stirred in what spices he had. "Not much of a dinner, boys, but it will have to do. Unless one of us can spot something tastier as we go, it's going to be hardtack and dried stew all the way there and back."

"We cannot spare the powder, nor dare we advertise our presence so boldly," Howe replied. "What we have fetched along will just have to serve to satisfy Joseph's stomach."

Joseph, to his credit, did not groan, and set down the wood he'd gathered beside the campfire, then crouched to warm his hands.

"Do you reckon, then, that the Mohawk are nearby, sergeant?"

"I should hope not, but if they were, we would know naught of it until they wished to announce their presence."

"Are they so difficult to spot in these woods?"

"They are like smoke, Joseph, and they have lived in these woods for many hundreds of years, at the least, so they have learned all the ways of keeping out of sight and covering their tracks. Those who dismiss them as primitive men or mere savages do so at their peril. The Indians I have known are as clever as you or William."

"That's not saying much, in Joseph's case," William said, with a guffaw. Joseph favored him with a sour look, and then turned back to Howe.

"I've heard that the Congress sought to make a pact with these Mohawk fellows, before the British convinced them to take up their side in the war. Is there any chance of turning them over to our side?"

"Well, Joseph, it's far more complicated than all that. Strictly speaking, the Mohawks are just one tribe of the Six Nations of the Iroquois Federation. They are probably the most warlike against our cause, but the rest save the Oneida have been doing the will of their British allies, spreading death and destruction across this part of the frontier for several years."

"Sounds like whatever the General's got planned for them, they have coming to them."

"I believe that the Congress is acting in the hope that this action is sufficient to bring the Iroquois back to neutrality in this struggle, or to at least splinter the Iroquois further. The Onondaga and the Tuscarora tribes may be amenable to alliance, if we can but convince them that to oppose us means their certain destruction."

William looked up from where he stirred their meager stew. "What is your experience of these tribes, sergeant?"

"I have but little direct experience of them, William. The Oneida, of course, you've seen at the garrison, and the Mohawk are their kin, but have their own distinct ways, naturally."

Howe finished with the waxcloth, pinning down the ends with rocks he'd found in a nearby moraine. Standing, he continued, "You'll see your fill of their ways tomorrow, if we can pick up our pace just a bit."

He peered up through the multicolored canopy of dripping leaves and added, "Of course, that would be considerably easier if this rain would cease."

Joseph grunted in agreement, as he sat on a large log he had dragged into the clearing for all three men to sit on before the fire pit. "So long as it doesn't turn to snow before we've gone from this place for home, I'll be well-enough satisfied. Is that stew ready, William?"

William shook his head and rolled his eyes as he lifted the pot off the fire with a stout branch. "Can always trust you to be thinking with your stomach, can't we? Where's your plate?"

Darkness settled deeply over the woods as the three chewed the stringy stew, each lost in their own thoughts. The only sound came from the spatter of the rain dripping upon all as the smoke from the dying campfire rose straight upward in the still night air.

Chapter 3

Tanarou was deeply frustrated. Not only was the ground wet with the night's rain, but his young companion lay nearby, facing the sky with his mouth flung wide open, and deep, resounding snores sounding from within his throat.

The old warrior's mind was already full enough with concern over the implications of the Colonial party they'd spied that morning, and sleep would have been elusive under the best of circumstances, but between worry, rain and racket, there seemed little chance that he would get any rest this night.

He rolled onto his side and listened to what he could hear of the noises of the night over the drone of Ginawo's snoring. It sounded as though the rain were stopping, and he could discern the quiet hoot of a distant owl, calling out his territory to all who would disturb it.

Tanarou wondered why the People seemed to have to so often yield their territory, rather than standing and claiming it as did the owl, the wolf, or the fox. His grandfather's generation had been forced to give up a warm and friendly land, and the stories of the ancestors spoke of prior journeys that the People had been forced into over the ages.

And now, he worried, the time was again coming that they would have to yield to the forces of the world. If the Colonials applied their massed power to the People, his village would again need to carry their children and elders, build lodges, clear fields and learn the dangers and opportunities of a new land.

Tanarou shook his head angrily and threw his arm over his ear, trying to clear his mind and lure sleep to his side. No amount of worry would stop the events which were already in motion about him, and only a bear hide would silence the youth nearby.

When the morning broke the next day, Tanarou had managed enough rest to awaken before Ginawo. He arose from the hard ground and reached for his moccasins, seeking to release the knotted muscle and sinew of his back. Once he'd stretched out the stiffness of the night, he prodded Ginawo with his toe.

"Rise, winter bear," he said. "You have growled the night away, and frightened breakfast into flight."

"I have done no such thing, revered elder," Ginawo said, rubbing the night grit from his eyes.

"It sounded like lake ice driven before a great wind in spring, all night," rejoined Tanarou. "Any creature that remained within hearing of this place last night would be considering us for its meal, and would be nothing that feared us. Also, you kept me from my sleep."

"I am sorry for that, respected elder. I would not want to deprive you of either rest or food, knowing that a lack of either makes you poor company in the morning."

Tanarou gave the younger man the sour look he'd been seeking, and Ginawo grinned merrily at him as he rose. Rather than continuing to spar with his companion, Tanarou turned away and gathered up his blankets silently.

Ginawo did likewise, and took Tanarou's burden into his own basket, which he strapped onto his back without comment.

He saw that, despite trying to keep his expression dour, the older man had a twinkle of merriment in his own eye.

Striding into the forest without further preparation, Tanarou said over his shoulder, "We will be at the village by the middle of the day." Almost more to himself than to his companion, he continued, "I shall have to call a council of the elders, and persuading them of the seriousness of this threat will be difficult."

He sighed. "There will be those who would stay, even as a squirrel will retreat to his tree as the fire approaches. By the time he recognizes that the danger cannot be ignored, it is too late to flee, and the squirrel perishes in the flames."

Ginawo answered, "How can you tell the squirrel that his tree offers only death?"

Tanarou grunted. "By making a smarter squirrel." Shaking his head, he said, "No, we must let those who would try to hide in place feel the tree shake, so that they may come to understand that it offers no safety."

He came to a decision then, continuing, "You shall accompany me to the council and tell them directly what we saw, and what they said. The pale men do not see our People as being different from our clan-brothers, and those of our brothers who think that we can drive all of them from these lands forever have awakened a rage in these Colonials that I fear will break upon us all. Perhaps if the council hears this from your own mouth, in the very words of the Colonial men we found, they will be persuaded."

Ginawo said nothing, but Tanarou could see his throat working as the younger man swallowed hard in a nervous gesture familiar to all who knew him.

"Do not worry, Ginawo. There are none in the council who

would treat you with disrespect, and indeed your skills have been the subject of considerable discussion among certain of the elders."

He did not share with the younger man the considered opinion of the council that, with some added maturity, Ginawo had the potential to be a great leader of the People, between his gift of memory and his inborn strength. He lacked the proper respect for his elders, and had a knack of being incautious at inopportune moments, of course, but these imperfect traits would fade with time.

Uncharacteristically, Ginawo did not ask Tanarou what he had meant by his comment, and the older man took that as a sign that some of the needed maturity might even now be manifesting itself.

The pair had been walking for some while when Tanarou stopped suddenly, signally with his hand for Ginawo to be silent. Reaching over his shoulder, Tanarou pulled his bow from where it was slung, and notched an arrow in total silence.

Ginawo watched without moving at all as Tanarou drew back his bow, and aimed carefully. Uttering a completely convincing imitation of a turkey hen's call, he paused for a moment and then loosed his arrow at his unseen quarry. Tanarou grunted in satisfaction as a burst of sound marked the impact of his shot.

Flapping in its death-throes, a young tom turkey lurched into Ginawo's line of site, and the younger man relaxed as Tanarou looked over his shoulder at him, a pleased smile on his face.

Ginawo was suitably impressed—despite the older man's comparison of him yesterday to a drunken turkey, he knew that they were wily birds, and that they were able to see nearly all the way around themselves. Fooling even a young tom into being still enough to get a good shot at it was a feat, even for a man of Taranou's years and experience.

Re-slinging the bow on his back, Tanarou walked forward and silenced the large bird, snapping its neck to bring its struggles to an end. He bent to retrieve his arrow from the animal's back, and then picked up the bird by its feet and handed it over to Ginawo.

"You may carry it into the village—perhaps Jiwaneh will be impressed." He gave the younger man a sly grin, and then continued, "It will be good to at least bring some food with us to soften the bad news we deliver."

Ginawo hefted the bird and then set it down, pulling his knife from its sheath to begin cleaning the animal. He made quick work of the task, and then used the blade to dig a small hole in which to bury the offal.

Tanarou watched, nodding with approval at the careful work that the younger man put into the routine chore. Tying the bird's feet into his pack harness, Ginawo slung the carcass over his shoulder and then carefully cleaned the blade of his knife on a handful of wet leaves. He dropped them into the hole atop the offal, and then bent to scoop the soil back into the hole.

"That will do, Ginawo, very nicely indeed." Tanarou added skill in assisting, at least, with the hunt to the mental list of Ginawo's merits that he had begun to make note of.

By the time that the sun had burned off the morning clouds and began to dapple the ground through the still-damp leaves overhead, Tanarou's keen nose had already picked up the scents of home. He smelled smoke from the cooking fires, the aroma of open earth where the fall crops yet grew, and soon heard the shouts of children at play.

Rounding a gentle curve in the well-worn track leading into the village, he was gratified to see that all was as they had left it and he couldn't help but wonder for how long it would remain so.

There would be time for such thoughts later, when the council could meet in the extended longhouse at the center of the village. For now, Tanarou was content to see Ginawo's favorite Jiwaneh, take note of the younger man's arrival, and of the bird he carried.

She did not rise from where she worked, gathering the last of the squash from the field, but he could see her eyes follow Ginawo's form through the village over to old Hawakeke, who took the bird from him after he untied it from the strap upon his shoulder.

Tanarou noted, too, that Ginawo's eyes darted over to where Jiwaneh worked as he handed the carcass over to the old woman. He smiled inwardly, congratulating himself for the tiny deception in Ginawo's favor.

He could see the younger man gesturing over to where he stood, doubtless explaining that he was not, himself, to credit for the prize, but Hawakeke still grasped his shoulder and thanked Ginawo for the food on behalf of the village. She then turned and handed it to a younger girl to pluck and ready for cooking, and Tanarou signaled Ginawo to rejoin him.

Together, the two men entered the lodge, pausing for a moment at the threshold to permit their eyes time to adjust to the sudden darkness of its interior. Once he could see by the dim light of the small fire in the center firepit of the three inside the long lodge, Tanarou advanced to where Nitchawake dozed.

Standing before the aged old warrior, Tanarou waited patiently for Nitchawake to note his presence and to invite him to speak. As he waited, Tanarou studied the old man's face. As usual, his skin and hair were colored darkly with the costly dye procured from the old homeland out of which the People had most recently been forced.

In the dim light of the lodge, the old man's skin looked almost like the shell of a butternut, a rich and dark reddish-brown. Tanarou could see the worry lines etched into Nitchawake's face, and wondered whether his own face was not becoming similarly lined with the concerns of his era in turn.

As Tanarou waited, Karowenna's voice came out of the shadows in the far corner of the lodge. "You do not return looking any happier than when you left, Tanarou. You have learned something new of our perilous situation?"

"I have, yes, revered elder," Tanarou answered. Nitchawake's eyes opened, alert, and the old man raised a hand to motion to Tanarou to continue.

"While Ginawo and I were watching near the place where the three streams join on a hill, we encountered a scouting party of pale men. They wore the clothing of the Colonials, and Ginawo heard them speak of a large party of warriors to come. I believe that we must gather a council of the elders and consider whether we should abandon the village."

Nitchawake's eyebrows raised at this last comment, and Tanarou bore on, "We know that our clan-brothers have raided and burned the villages of the Colonials. I do not think that it is too much to imagine that they might seek to bring the same destruction down upon us."

Karowenna spoke up again, hissing from the darkness, "They cannot believe that our clan-brothers will be influenced to put down their war-clubs by attacking the villages of the People!"

Nitchawake finally spoke, his low, raspy voice difficult to hear even so close by. "The pale men do not think in the same way as we do. They have not the ties of clan, but only the divisions of tribe. They cannot understand that attacking one tribe for the war brought to them by another tribe will not split the tribes from one another, but will only awaken the anger of clan-brothers."

He sat up fully now, turning to face Karowenna where she lay. "I agree that Tanarou is wise to ask the council to act, and that the pale men could easily equate the People with our more warlike clan-brothers, or even believe that by attacking us, they can cause all of the Haudenosaunee to set aside their war-clubs."

Karowenna said nothing, and Tanarou could feel her eyes boring into him, though he could yet see nothing of her.

"I will summon the council," Tanarou said, adding, "I would bring Ginawo into the council to repeat in the pale men's own words what he heard." He indicated the silent younger man, who still stood by the entrance to the lodge, ready to speak to the elders if he were needed

Nitchawake nodded, and said, "We have heard much of this young warrior, and I believe that his talents will assist our council in its deliberations. You have done well, Tanarou, and the People are in your debt for the service you and your young friend have done us today."

"Thank you, revered elder. I only do what I can for the good of the People."

Tanarou turned and went outside, where the daylight blinded him for a moment. When his eyes adjusted again to the difference between the inside of the lodge and the light outdoors, he smiled for a moment to see Ginawo making a beeline to speak with Jiwaneh.

The young warrior and his favorite maiden made a striking couple, and since Jiwaneh was of the Turtle Clan, not the Bear Clan like Ginawo and himself, there was no barrier to their marriage, should they choose to continue their pursuit of one another.

Tanarou would miss the bright presence of the younger man once he moved to the lodge of Jiwaneh's mother, if the pair wed, but he could foresee a bright future for the two, with many strong children. Tanarou sighed, and turned to the warrior's lodge to find a swift messenger he could send to gather the elders.

Chapter 4

Sergeant Howe and his two men could see a large break in the crown of the woods ahead, and all three walked with great care, striving for absolute silence, that they might avoid alerting the Indian villagers ahead. Creeping from tree to tree, they advanced until they could see the fields and structures, and the villagers going about their daily business.

Howe noted carefully the location of the various lodges, sketching quickly with a stick of charcoal the layout of the village. He noted that the track into the south end of the clearing appeared to continue on through the village, leading to another that led into the north from the far side of the village, as well as the relative elevation of the surrounding terrain and the thickness of the forest from different approaches.

Joseph's eyes were wide as he took in every detail he could about the activities of the villagers. In the fields, he could see the stripped stalks of corn being pulled out of the ground and gathered up by a young woman, who then brought them inside the nearby longhouse. Meanwhile, three older women followed behind her and gathered the last of the squash that lay about on their vines.

In the center of the village, two strong men worked together, dressing the carcass of an elk. They were stripping the hide from the body carefully, rolling it and trimming excess fat from the inside of it as they went. An old woman tended a fire nearby, and supervised a trio of younger women as they prepared a rack of wood, upon which he reckoned they would soon dry the flesh of the animal to store it for the winter.

Joseph could not help but lick his lips at the sight of the fresh meat so close by, but he knew that it would have to remain out of his reach, at least for the time being. The wind shifted, and he wrinkled his nose at the sharp smell of fish drying inside one of the longhouses.

For his part, William was observant of the characteristics of the construction employed in the village. He felt sure that the bark outer covering on the longhouses could easily enough be fired, if the need arose, and they would burn quickly once alight.

The abbreviated palisade that surrounded a portion of the clearing would present little impediment to the advance of a large and determined force, and might even assist an invading army with containing the villagers within for capture, if the entrances could but be sealed.

Howe completed his sketched map and turned to the two privates, nodding to them and indicating with a flick of his eyes that they should move back away from the village now.

Joseph gazed over the bustling scene before them one last time as the scout group departed, and felt a stirring of disquiet at what the intelligence they were gathering might bring to pass. He could not help but notice the children scampering around, sometimes aiding their elders, but just as often pursuing their own ends. They reminded him of his nephews and nieces back at home in Pennsylvania.

Before enlisting in the Continental Army, he often had passed a pleasant afternoon playing with the children of his kin, and he realized that he disliked the thought of regarding these children here as potential military targets. He knew, of course, that the Indians had demonstrated no compunctions about slaughtering the children of settlers in the recent spate of attacks along the frontiers nearby, but he didn't see that such savagery on the part of their enemies made it acceptable to do likewise themselves.

Even after the three men were a safe distance away from the village, none seemed particularly inclined to chatter. Eventually, Howe called William over as they walked.

"William, what notes can you add to this map?"

Howe offered the page to William, who examined it closely. "The palisades extend more northward than you've indicated, I think. Everything in the village, of course, is susceptible to fire, and somewhere within the longhouses will be a considerable store of food that they've put aside for winter."

He considered for a moment longer. "If we should find it necessary to act against this village, I believe that we may most effectively do so by first positioning a force along the track to the north, and then moving the main force in from the south. As they enter the village, the northern flankers can close in and retard the escape of the Indians."

He handed the paper back to Howe, who nodded in approval of the other man's analysis. "Private, I do believe that you are hoping to earn a promotion to a higher rank soon, with that sort of strategic consideration."

William smiled and ducked his head slightly in acknowledgement of the sergeant's praise. "I have read the accounts of the French and Indian war, sir, and have drawn my lessons from what I could learn of the tactics employed in that contest."

"Well, you have learned your lessons well, and I shall ensure that the Lieutenant hears of it." Turning to Joseph, he asked, "Have you anything to add to William's analysis, Joseph?"

"I agree that they will have a lot of food stored up. I saw corn that had been harvested already, and there was squash being put up as we watched. I expect that they've put aside a fair amount of dried meat for the winter, too."

"I confess that I am not surprised that the study of their food supply should most occupy your attention, Joseph, but your observations are, of course, also of great value." He nodded, and rolled up the map sketch with a satisfied air.

"We must return now with all possible haste with this intelligence. We might have taken our leisure at times on the way here, but I am certain that this information is exactly what the General needs in order to make a decision as to how to deal with these Iroquois."

Joseph groaned, "When, exactly, did we take our leisure on the trip north? I do not think that we can take any less leisure than this journey has entailed. Naught from naught leaves less than naught, the way I figure it."

Howe grinned at him, "You shall see soon enough, Joseph, just how much leisure you had previously had. By the time we rejoin the General's army, you may well have enough reason to really groan."

Howe proved the truth of his words over the next several hours, pushing himself and his men hard on their return southward. The track was somewhat familiar to them now, and even Howe had a wistful moment when they passed by their encampment from the morning, but they slowed for only a few minutes at noon for hardtack and a mouthful of water.

He couldn't help but take note, though, of the beauty of the land that they passed through. There were frequent small streams, which, he thought, would provide reliable irrigation to farms, and abundant wildlife would ensure a steady supply of meat for the tables of those fortunate enough to settle in these lands, once the conflict ended.

Howe knew that he was unlikely to be awarded a land grant unless he were promoted to officer, but he still looked at the passing terrain with the eye of a hopeful future settler. Of course, some allowance would probably have to be made for some of the Indians—their allies the Oneidas, if no others, but Howe knew that historically, the Indians had readily made way for settlers in the long run. In any event, the Oneida homeland lay to the east of where they were now, he believed.

As the group forded yet another babbling stream, splashing through the icy water as quickly as possible that they might not soak through their leathern boots, Howe heard the shrill call of a bird unfamiliar to his ears. Immediately afterward, William cried out, and Howe whirled around to see that an arrow had sprouted from between the man's shoulder blades as he dropped to his knees, his eyes immediately rolling upward in his head.

Dropping to one knee beside him, Joseph already had his musket off his shoulder and had begun loading it when he, too, was struck with an arrow. Unlike William, though, he did not fall to the ground in stillness, but instead dropped his gun and roared in rage as he grabbed the shaft of the arrow where it emerged from the meaty part of his upper arm.

Howe threw himself prone and made his way over to Joseph,

pulling him down, as well, and placed his hand over the injured man's mouth and glared him into silence until he nodded. Taking the partially-loaded musket, Howe quickly finished tamping the charge and checked the lock to be sure that it was properly loaded with powder, before raising the smooth stock to his cheek.

Sighting down the long bore, Howe searched the forest behind them for any hint of movement, but neither saw nor heard anything. After the span of many wild heartbeats, he concluded that the attack was over and permitted himself to believe that they were not all to be scalped in this place.

There must have been at least two who attacked, otherwise there would have been no reason for the call he'd heard. However, if there had been a full war party, they would have already charged Howe's tiny command with war axes and clubs, intent on finishing the attack with outright butchery. Reasoning that the attack must now be over, and their assailants fled, he lowered the musket from his shoulder and willed himself to at least the appearance of calmness.

Scrabbling over the loose, damp leaves of the forest floor, he reached William's prone form and checked the man's neck for the pulse of life. There was nothing to feel there, though, and Howe sighed deeply as he reached up and closed the man's eyes. He unbuckled and dragged he dead man's pack over to where Joseph was stifling groans of pain.

"Be still," Howe hissed, as he tore away the stout fabric of Joseph's shirt from the blood-soaked rip started where the arrow had passed through. Howe slid his fingers around to check whether the point of the arrow had penetrated through to the other side, but found no further injury there.

Tugging at the arrow, Howe was surprised and gratified when it slid out of the wound cleanly, revealing a hardened wooden tip, rather than the barbed flint head he'd seen on the arrows of the Iroquois he was familiar with. As he cast the arrow aside, he noted that the wound bled profusely, but did not spurt—a good sign.

"You were born to be hanged, Joseph. Be still a moment longer, and hold pressure on the wound for a second while I ready a bandage."

Joseph gritted his teeth and nodded, reaching up with his good hand to apply pressure. Blood still flowed between his fingers, but it was a sluggish trickle now, already slowing as the damaged flesh began to close up.

Howe rummaged through the dead man's pack for a spare shirt, and then pulled out his own knife to cut a wide strip from it. "Move your hand now, Joseph. Poor William won't be needing this any more," he remarked, wadding up a bit of it to serve as a bandage, and then tying the rest over the wound gently but firmly.

Joseph looked away from where Howe was physicking his arm, and gazed at the dead man's form. He said, suddenly, "We can't leave him here, sergeant. They'll desecrate his corpse, take trophies and whatnot, maybe even take his scalp to sell to the British."

"What tales have you been listening to, Joseph? Do you purpose to carry him all the way back to New-Jersey? No, we must strip him of anything ourselves that they could make use of, and then fly as fast as ever we can in order that his death may be properly avenged."

Seeing Joseph's stricken expression, Howe continued, more

gently, "I know that he was a friend to you, and I am sorry for the need, but his sacrifice will be for naught if we cannot deliver to the General the intelligence which we purchased at the price of William's life."

Joseph took a long, shuddering breath and nodded. "I know we have to, but it still don't seem right to just leave him here. Can we at least give him a Christian burial?"

"No, Joseph. The longer we stay here, indeed, the more likely it is that whoever shot the two of you will return with a greater force to destroy us all. Can you stand?"

Joseph raised himself with his good arm and slowly struggled to his feet. Howe was already at William's side, pulling off his musket, boots, canteen and other gear. After donning the dead man's bag across his shoulder, he slung the gun across the opposite shoulder from his own. The rest of the gear he stuffed into his and William's sacks, which now counterbalanced each other across his shoulders.

"Do you want a sling to keep from jostling that arm?"

"Nay, I am able to move as it is now." Taking one last sad glance at the shocking sight of his companion's body where it lay sprawled across the fallen leaves, under the brilliant canopy of autumn, Joseph fell in behind the sergeant's quick, purposeful strides away from the scene of their loss.

Chapter 5

O nce again the elders gathered in the great longhouse, the mood grimmer even than the last time they had met. Once the ceremonial drums marking the beginning of the conclave had finished, Tanarou stood and spoke without waiting for any further ritual.

"My companion Ginawo and I have learned of the advance into our homeland of a force of the Colonials. We know not what their purpose may be for this incursion, but I believe that it is not unreasonable to assume that they do not travel in force merely to present belts or other tokens of peace."

He looked around at the deeply-lined faces around the fire, each of them well-known to him over many seasons of serious consideration of the best decisions possible to ensure that the People should survive, and even thrive. Taking a deep breath, he continued, "I believe that the only choice open to us at this time is to follow the example of the fox when fire sweeps the land, and abandons his den until after the danger has passed."

The assembled elders stirred, but nobody stood to interrupt him. "We must fade like a mist into the woods and return when the Colonials have left these lands."

Hotoke rose now, his eyes narrowed in anger and his nostrils flared with passion. "You would have us slink into the shadows while these pale men range over our homeland unanswered?"

He glared directly at Tanarou now, his eyes flashing. "Have you not heard the words on the wind, Tanarou? You are right about one thing—the Colonials have not come to offer anything but death and destruction."

Turning now to address the elders as a group, he continued, his voice rising, "I have spoken with some of my clan-brothers of the Wolf whose villages they have burned, whose children they have taken captive, whose fields they have destroyed."

Returning his attention to Tanarou, he concluded, "Before this threat you would have us hide? I thought that bears stood tall and strong before their enemies. Are you sure that you are not truly a Turtle, Tanarou?"

Tanarou inhaled sharply at the last comment, as did Karowenna. The old woman's voice rang out across the fire, "You should not speak so dismissively of the Turtle clan, Hotoke. We have fought always with tenacity and bravery, and your words are ill-considered. You should leave this circle now and consider your words more carefully in the future."

With a look of disgust, Hotoke turned without another word and strode out of the lodge. After he was gone, Karowenna sighed and stood up. "While I do not like the way in which Hotoke chose to say it, I know that he speaks for many among the People. It is not our way to run when a challenge presents itself."

She turned to face Tanarou now, continuing, "I agree with Tanarou, however, that this is a situation where the urge to stand and fight would lead to the destruction of everything we are. The pale men, assembled in great numbers, will overrun us, and they will kill or capture those who stand before them. Better to lose the den than the cubs; better the cubs than the entire family."

She drew herself up to her full height, undiminished despite her many years. "Yes, I am of the Turtle clan, and as one who has always found solace in the strength of the turtle's armored back, I am not pleased at all to see this day come. Yet if we attempt to stay put in the face of this threat, we will be washed away, as the turtle who fails to anticipate the flood."

Tanarou spoke again. "Hotoke's news is as I had feared when Ginawo and I found these scouts of the pale men's army. We have spoken in this very council of the destruction wreaked upon the villages of the pale men by our clan brothers and the blood-jackets, working together. Is it a surprise to any of us here that they should now sweep across the lands of the Haudenosaunee to avenge their losses?"

He grimaced. "Long have we heard the counsel of our respected elders that we ought to remain apart from this conflict between the two tribes of the pale men, and much have we decried the decisions of many of our clan brothers to ignore this wisdom. Now, it appears that we all will together pay the price for the warlike ways of a few."

An elder from a minor village to the west, Tikorenu, spoke up now. "Do you propose that all of the villages of the People should be emptied, that we find some way to survive the coming winter, without the warmth of our lodges, without the food we have stored, without the safety of our village walls?"

"If we stay, we are a stone to be overturned; if we go, we are the water that flows onward." Tanarou again grimaced. "In their rage, the pale men will burn our lodges, whether they shelter us or not. They will destroy our crops, whether we remain to hunger for them or not. They will knock down our walls, whether we lie beneath them or not."

He gestured to the circle, and, by extension, to all who lay beyond it. "Lodges, fields, walls, these we can rebuild in a single season, once the anger of the pale men is spent. If we stay, we may not survive to rebuild anything at all. Yes, all of the villages of the People must be empty when the pale men come to them."

Nitchawake finally spoke, and all assembled listened intently. "It is as Tanarou has said. We can stay to fight and be utterly extinguished, or we can leave and return when the pale men have exhausted their anger upon our possessions."

He sighed and continued, "We must, however, consider whether we can prevent this fate from falling upon us again. Some here have indeed counseled that we remain apart from this fight, however, it is my feeling that the fight will not remain apart from us. We may yet have to choose a side to ally ourselves with."

He waved his hands to dispel the angry murmur that arose on all sides. "This is not what we must decide today, however. Right now, we must decide how to avoid being drowned in the coming flood. I say we move for higher ground, uncomfortable though that ground may be."

Karowenna again spoke. "It must be as our brother Tanarou has said. Our villages must be emptied, and all that can be carried away brought with us. We can find shelter in the ways of our mothers and aunts, and we can find sustenance from the lands that we pass through as we flee. Do any yet disagree?"

None spoke, and Nitchawake said, "So is the decision of this conclave to be recorded in the songs of our children, then. We chose to save the lives of the People when the anger of the pale men threatened to sweep us away. The elders of each of the villages are, as is our custom, welcome to come to their own decisions, based on the wisdom of their mothers, but this village will be emptied."

The drums and cries of the ceremonies marking the end of the conclave sounded more somber and mournful than Ginawo had ever heard before, and as the group exited the lodge, he could hear the warriors and the women being given their tasks already to prepare the village for flight.

Jiwaneh ran to Ginawo when she saw him emerge from the lodge. "It is true, then, that we are to take to the forests, that the pale men are coming to burn and kill?"

Ginawo replied, "That is what they have begun to do already to the east and south of here, we have learned, yes. We will give them nobody to kill, and only some worthless empty lodges to burn for their entertainment. Stay close to me as we flee, and I will ensure that no harm befalls you."

He looked into the young woman's eyes. "I shall speak to your mother of this when the storm of the pale men has passed, but I wish to see to it that no harm comes to you... ever."

She held his gaze, her eyes welling up with emotion. "I will feel safe under your protection, Ginawo, today and all days. You need fear nothing of my mother, that much I can say with confidence."

He smiled tenderly at her, and only Tanarou's shout from across the central clearing of the village broke the spell between them. Ginawo bounded over to the older man, his mind clearly on other things than the tasks immediately before them.

Tanarou shook his head, smiling at the young man's joy in the midst of this disaster for the People. "I see that you have indeed found your straight-limbed maiden in Jiwaneh. I am glad that you have discovered something to derive joy from as we prepare for the time of smoke, yet we have serious matters to attend to."

Ginawo, slightly chastised, nodded, his face turning ever so slightly pink. He was not ordinarily shy around Tanarou, but something about this moment felt different to him. "I shall attend to my duties, honored elder."

"Good. That is all that is required of you. Soon, it seems, you will have duties of your own, but for the moment, your duties are to the People."

Ginawo nodded soberly, and Tanarou was reminded strongly of himself at the same age. It had also been a time of war, although that one had seen the British and Colonials fighting together against the French.

"I know what it is to feel the pull of a girl, even as the clouds of war swirl about the People. I was not always an elder; I did not spring from the Earth with lines on my face. When I was a young warrior, the fight was against the Algonquin and the French, and again the People were pulled into an alliance with the British."

His expression saddened as he continued, "Because I neglected one set of duties in favor of another, I lost much that mattered to me. I would not see you suffer the same fate, my young friend."

Ginawo nodded, in wonder at what pain could bring a brightness to the eyes of a man who had ever been a steady oak in his presence before, but unwilling to inquire more closely.

"What do the People require of me at this moment, honored elder?" For once, there was no mocking in Ginawo's tone, and as Tanarou began listing the tasks that needed to be accomplished, he felt a new respect and closeness for his mentor. There was much work to do.

The Smoke

Chapter 6

Weary and worn, Joseph and Sergeant Howe spotted the van of the approaching army and made themselves known to the men at the lead when they were challenged. Within a the space of a what seemed like little more than few minutes, they were walking with the lieutenant, who wore an expression of grave concern at seeing Joseph's wound and noting William's absence.

"You came under attack? Were you seen at the village, then?"

"Nay, sir," Howe replied. "We succeeded in our mission to gather intelligence on the village, and were bound for the south when we were ambushed by a force unknown."

He motioned to Joseph, beside him, continuing, "Private Holder was killed instantly by an arrow fired from our rear, and Private Killeen, as you can see, was wounded in the same action. Killeen and I did seek to return fire, but the Indians who struck did not present themselves at any time. We were forced to abandon Private Holder's corpse, in the interest of ensuring the safe delivery of this map to your hand."

With that, Howe placed the rolled map that he had worked out with William into the Lieutenant's hand.

"Did you see any indication of the identity of the Indians who attacked you?"

"Only the arrows, sir, both of which were typical of the Iroquois' weaponry in every respect save one. The one that I removed from Private Killeen's arm had no head attached to it, but consisted only of a hardened wooden point. That struck me as passing odd, but I could not spare the time to reflect further upon it."

The Lieutenant nodded. "I wish that I could seek the counsel of our Oneida friends on this, but not everyone trusted them to be reliable companions as we moved against their fellow Iroquois confederates. However, Sergeant Snelling may be able to advise us as to whether we may learn anything from this detail."

He unrolled the map and examined it for a moment. As he rolled it back up, Howe spoke, saying, "Private Holder believed that it might be possible to pen the Indians of this village in from the north before we attacked from the south. I concur, and hope that we may be able to make use of his insights when we reach our objective."

The Lieutenant opened the map again and studied it with more attention. "We're still some thirty miles distant from this village, is that right?"

"Aye, 'tis probably another four days' march, more if the weather interferes, or if we have other duties along the way."

"Our march will be the General's decision, but I shall see to it that this intelligence reaches his hands as soon as possible. Private Killeen should go now to the surgeon to have that arm looked at."

"Oh, it will be just fine, Lieutenant," Joseph said, quickly. The surgeon was best known for his collection of bone saws, and none visited him, save for when the stench of gangrene had become undeniable.

"I know a private in the company who is a skilled hand with poultices, and has a lot of experience at drawing out infection before it ever has a chance to settle into a wound," Howe added. He likewise had no desire to see Joseph pay the surgeon a visit, unless the need were urgent.

The Lieutenant raised his hand and nodded. "Very well; seek the remedies you see fit to use." He frowned. "However, if the wound turns ill, I expect you to avail yourself of the services offered to you by this army, rather than let it fester until we must appoint a detail to dig your grave."

Joseph swallowed visibly. "I do understand, sir, and I shall not let it reach that point in any event."

"Good. Take your rest, then. Tell the quartermaster that I said that you two are to ride in the wagon for the balance of the day, to regain your strength. Private, I would see you in the morning to examine your wound, please."

"Yes, sir." As they turned away from the officer to find the quartermaster and the blessed relief of a few hours off their feet in his wagon, Joseph could not help but permit a scowl to cross his face. Was he not to be trusted with his own well-being?

Sergeant McDonahugh was none too pleased to let the two men clamber aboard his supply wagon, even when Howe told him that it was at the Lieutenant's orders.

"Aye, but 'tis not the Lieutenant's horses that draw this wagon, is it? Oh, but he'll hear from me on this, he will."

Howe and Joseph did their best to ignore the quartermaster's fulmination and bluster, and before long, they both snored atop the bundled supplies, as the wagon bounced over rock and twig alike along the rough track.

They slept still when the quartermaster ordered his horses to a halt, even before the sun had set. Howe sat up and rubbed the grit from his eyes. He called out, "Sergeant, what cause has the army to draw up short of our goal for the day?"

"Ye will have missed the word, won't ye've, that we stop for every little Indian village our scouts locate. We're to destroy all in our path, and send what prisoners we can take back to Fort Sullivan to be held. General Washington means to end the Iroquois threat in these parts for good, that we may return to fighting the lobsterbacks directly, rather than through their Indian proxies."

Howe absorbed this information, then nodded. "I have heard much of the cruelty of the Iroquois raids in this country, and I confess that I am little surprised to learn that this is now the official policy of this army. We have found a village nearby, then?"

"Indeed, though it hardly seems worth flattening. The scouts report that it is scarcely occupied, and the fields in poor repair." The quartermaster shrugged. "Ours is not to question the General's orders, however, but only to hop to when he says so."

Gesturing at the still-slumbering Joseph, he continued, "Speaking of, 'tis high time that you two remove yourselves from my supplies, and stir about, until you can take your leisure in the encampment."

Howe nodded after a moment, and reached over to prod Joseph. "Up you go, Joseph, easy now."

As the wounded man awoke and grunted in pain for trying to raise himself on the bandaged arm, Howe asked, "Will you be able to come down from here unaided?"

Gritting his teeth, Joseph answered, "Aye, but a tot of rum or whiskey would not be taken amiss, I think. This arm now hurts more than it did when I was shot."

"Aye, laddie, 'tis the way of most wounds that they bring more pain after resting than they did upon the initial hurt," the quartermaster said, offering his meaty hand to the young man.

"I've some whiskey in my private stores that I'll share with ye gladly enough, and we can see about a fresh bandage, too."

"I am most grateful for your care, Sergeant."

"'Tis nothing, laddie. I am but pleased that you no longer ride upon my stores." He smiled at the private. "'Tis nothing personal, laddie, but the Lieutenant forgets that I am not a carriage service. We will be here until nightfall while the detachment destroys the village we've found, and we'll doubtless encamp for the night."

"There's to be action, then?" Joseph's agitation was obvious on his face.

Howe noted his upset and said, soothingly, "Yes, Joseph, but we'll take no part in today's fight. 'Tis but a small village, which will not be suffered to stand. I have learned while you slept that it is now the General's policy to make total war on the Iroquois of this territory."

Joseph interjected, "But there are children and women in those villages. Do we not spare the innocents among our enemies?"

Howe looked sharply at Joseph, and said in a harsh tone, "I cannot see but that the Iroquois have brought this upon themselves, having conducted unrestricted warfare upon the settlers in this frontier. Do not forget your own unfortunate neighbors—I misdoubt that their attackers discriminated between the sexes or ages of those people."

Joseph kept his counsel, but it was written upon his face that he did not like this new tactic in the war against the Indians. How could they hold themselves as being any better than their opponents, if they lowered themselves to the same level of reasoning?

McDonahugh came back at that moment, a tin cup in one hand and fresh bandages in the other. "Here, laddie, drink this, and once it's settled in your gut, we'll get clean bandages on you."

Joseph accepted the cup with a grateful nod and tossed it back. His face screwed tightly, but he did not choke as the liquor burned its way down his throat. After a moment, he opened his eyes again and handed the cup back to McDonahugh.

"Thank you," he managed to choke out, and then he turned to let the quartermaster work on his arm. Gritting his teeth against the waves of pain that washed over him despite the man's gentleness in unwrapping and re-bandaging the wound, Joseph found that he felt a good deal less compassion in this moment for the Indians whose doom approached.

Chapter 7

Tanarou looked on in approval as Ginawo pulled another strip of bark askew from the side of the lodge they were working on. The young warrior had suggested the ruse to Nitchawake, who had nodded thoughtfully.

"If we can make the village look as though it is mostly or completely abandoned, perhaps the pale men will not find it worth destroying." The old man shrugged, adding, "If we cannot fool them, then it makes little difference, as we will have to rebuild the entire village anyway, and what damage you inflict will be erased anyway."

A group of children ran, shrieking with laughter, through a nearby field, reveling in the freedom to intrude upon ground that was normally forbidden to them. Past the fields, a small group of warriors were tugging at some of the tree trunks that comprised the palisade surrounding the village.

Once the decision had been made to abandon the village to what depredations the pale men might choose to visit upon it, it was easy enough to convince the elders to undo years of careful, constant maintenance in a single, purposeful spree of self-destructive preservation.

Once he had accepted Ginawo's suggestion of creating a deceptive appearance of the village, the younger man then spoke to Nitchawake of the bolder portion of his proposal.

"Honored elder, it would be my privilege to stay while the People fly into the forests, and complete the illusion that this is a failing, poor settlement, hardly worth bothering with. I am certain that a few other warriors will gladly join me in this."

Nitchawake squinted into the distance, pondering for a long moment, before he responded. "To convince the pale men that we are failing and not fled, you will want at least one elder among your number, as well. I will stay with you, Ginawo."

The younger man paused before replying, taken aback at the old warrior's faith in him. "I will be deeply honored to share this duty with you, revered elder. If we cannot persuade them that our poor village is not worth their attention, then we can, perhaps, exact a price in blood from them for our destruction."

When Jiwaneh heard of the plan from another young warrior who was bragging to his fellows that he, too, would stand beside Ginawo, she dropped the basket of nearly-ripe squash she was carrying and strode to where Ginawo was directing the defacement of the clan totem over the door of one of the lodges.

She stood before him and cried, "How will you protect me always, if you sacrifice yourself in this reckless plan? If you are to throw your life away, I will speak plainly to you, Ginawo."

She wiped furious tears from her face, continuing, "I dream of raising your children to be strong and wise, and to follow in the footsteps of their father. I see myself sitting beside you at the end of our days, many seasons from now, taking our places among the revered elders of the People."

He placed gentle, comforting hands on her shoulders, and said softly, "We must do what we can to preserve the People, Jiwaneh. If the pale men find this place completely empty, they will as a matter of course leave it in ashes, and then seek the people who have flown before them. If they find it pitiable, perhaps they will take pity."

He nodded to the warriors secreting weapons inside the doorway of a nearby lodge. "And if not, I will hear their words, and we will strike them and fade into the woods while they writhe in confusion. If we take them by surprise, we will escape and join the rest of the village in the woods."

Drawing a long, shuddering breath, she said, "I will not wrap your corpse tomorrow and sing in lamentation with the drums. If you will stay here, then I will be with you, that this illusion should be all the more convincing. If they are fooled, I will be at your side; if you run, I will fly with you; if you fall, I will sleep beside you."

He regarded her for the span of a soaring hawk's lazy wingbeat, and then nodded. "You do know that I can no longer call myself a Bear, but will instead join your mother's clan of the Turtle when this crisis has passed."

She nodded back at him, her eyes still bright with tears. "I have known since last summer that you would come to live under the roof of my mother, and I was only waiting for you to see it yourself."

Jiwaneh motioned with her eyes to the elongated lodge in the center of the village, where the ceremonial fire lay. "We have not the time today for the drums of celebration, but I am certain now that we will live to hear them cry out in joy for us, and that we will together sing the songs of joining."

Ginawo drew her into her arms, and it was only then that she permitted herself to sob fully, if just for a few minutes. She mourned for the lost chance to enjoy the full courtship that they ought to have pursued together, and she grieved for the future that might well be swept away from them by the coming storm.

As the two young people embraced, Tanarou observed them from across the village clearing. He could read from the way they held each other all that had passed between them, as clearly as if it had been told to him in a story. Even while he exulted at the young warrior's initiative in the defense of the People, Tanarou felt a chill for the future that the young couple faced.

Turning back to the task of gathering up all that could be carried away and lashing it to the backs of a steady stream of the assembled villagers, Tanarou felt his mind drifting back to his own youth, when he, like Ginawo, had assumed upon himself a leadership role at a time of deep crisis.

The British King had sent his representative to meet with the Grand Council of the elders of the Haudenosaunee Confederation, bearing gifts and flattery, and seeking to renew the Covenenant Chain that had bound the People in alliance with the British, against the combined threat of the French and the Algonquin.

Tanarou had been a young man, and had traveled to the Grand Council as a companion to the revered elders of the People. He had stood at the entranceway of the lodge, just as he had lately invited Ginawo to do, and had been witness to the great debate.

One elder clan-brother, blind with his age, had stood and faced the British representative. "You would have us return to the ways of warfare, but can you ensure that our homes will remain safe from the incursions of your French clan-brothers?"

The British representative, a man who spoke the tongue of the People with a harsh accent but great clarity, replied, "Our great elder, King George, has conveyed to me that he will personally covenant to you that your homelands will be preserved for as long as he sits upon his throne, and he will likewise bind his heirs in this vow to you."

Another elder had snorted at this, muttering, "And when has the covenant of a pale man been worth the belt in which it was conveyed?" Aloud, he'd added, "Why does not your great elder bind his lesser elders among us to respect our prior covenants? What difference does it make to me or my clan-brothers whether the farms that appear within our homelands are peopled by settlers who speak your English or the enemy's French?"

The King's representative had paled as the elder spoke, but he quickly recovered and replied, "Will the French King or his Algonquin allies offer you any quarter as they encroach upon your homelands in the Ohio country? Indeed, they promise you only ruin and removal, and will ever continue their advance, unto the very elimination of the Haudenosaunee people."

He gestured in appeal to the assembled Council. "Will you not accept the gift of alliance with King George, and do what is possible to preserve your people? Would you turn this belt away and attempt to withstand the onslaught of the Algonquin peoples single-handed?"

Holding the fingers of one hand together with his other hand to illustrate his point, he continued, "Does your Confederation not derive strength from the combined efforts of your individual tribes, each of which would fall like a stalk of grass alone? Yet bound together by your Confederation, you are the strongest of the Indian nations in this land."

He folded his thumb into the grasp of his encircling hand

and concluded, "I pray that you will bind your strength together with ours, that together we can defeat the wickedness that threatens us from without."

He then sat down and waited for any member of the Grand Council to offer a further challenge to his proposal. The elected elder of the conclave finally stirred and spoke. "I see the wisdom of our British brother's words, and I dare to hope that his promises will be kept for all time. We must re-form the Covenant Chain of alliance with the British and together stand against the French and Algonquins."

He looked around the circle, meeting the eyes of each of the elders there assembled. "I know that many of you had hoped that we could stay out of this fight between the tribes of the pale men, that we could let their dispute pass over us like the winds over a field, that we could but bend in the breeze and let it crash upon the rocks."

He shook his head sadly. "This is not to be our fate, my brothers. If we do not renew the Covenant Chain, we will be wholly swept away, and never more to return to our homes. The decision is upon us; will any stand against it?"

The elders of the Grand Council shared many silent looks pregnant with meaning, but none spoke. "Very well, then. We will accept the belt offered by the British King George, and we will fight alongside you once again." He transfixed the British representative with his stare, adding, "We will fight together with you, but not again alone, and I trust that your King George will be a man of honor in his promises to us."

Tanarou had faded out through the entranceway at that point, readying the supplies of his tribe's elders for the return trip home.

Within days of their arrival back in their homeland, a raiding party of Algonquin had swept through the territory of the People, and Taranou's bride, she of the flashing eyes and straight limbs, had been taken, along with a double-handful of other women and children.

He remembered the earnest words of the British soldier, translated by a young warrior not unlike Ginawo, who assured him that they would do everything in their power to recover the kidnapped tribe members, and he remembered the sadness in the man's eyes as he returned to report that the Algonquin had escaped to the south.

He never heard anything of her fate, and even now, as he tied a load of corn to the back of a girl barely taller than the basket that held it, the ache in his heart was as keen as when he had been a smooth-faced young warrior himself. Glancing back over at Ginawo and Jiwaneh, he saw that they had released each other, and were engaged in sober discussion, the emotion of the moment now expended, and only practicalities remaining to be arranged.

Ginawo looked up then at Tanarou, and an unspoken understanding passed between the men. Theirs might be a desperate stand, but they would together preserve the hope for the future of the People represented by the new relationship just cemented in the whirlwind.

Chapter 8

The detachment returned, smelling of embers and mayhem as they passed the place where Howe and Joseph were still resting, near the quartermaster's wagon. The militiamen were dragging in their wake a small contingent of Indians. Dejected and filthy in appearance, Howe thought that they were the sorriest-looking lot of captives he'd ever imagined seeing.

He could hear the Lieutenant's voice carrying across the temporary encampment to the leader of the detachment as he strode toward the arriving column. "Any casualties, Sergeant Berkman?"

"We lost two men in an ambush the deceitful savages had set up for us. 'Twere the most ragged-looking village, hardly worth the effort to fire, and at first, the Indians made as though they were fleeing us. As soon as we began to raze it, though, they sprang up and begun to fight us. Took us off-guard, it did, but we were able to subdue them in short order."

Howe could see a thoughtful expression come over Berkman's face before the man continued, "I got the impression from the way the place went up with the fire that they had gone to some pains to render it shabby, and that the settlement was actually quite solid. Their deception availed them not, but we ought bear it in mind when we come to other villages in this campaign."

He nodded in the direction of the bound and dejected

captives. "I misdoubt that this were the entire population, either. We took no children, yet there were some signs that children had been about—little shoes and toys in some of the longhouses. I think that they must have had intelligence of our attack, and evacuated in advance of our arrival."

The Lieutenant looked at him sharply and said in a voice that scarcely carried to where Howe sat, "Do you think we have a spy among us, or that we are being observed from without?"

Berkman replied confidently, "I cannot imagine that we have any spy with us, but I do not doubt that they have observed our movements."

The Lieutenant nodded, satisfied. "Very well. How many did you kill, as opposed to capturing?"

"We killed but three, an aged man and two younger warriors, before the rest started a-jabbering, and then laid down their arms. They surrendered to our custody then and we took them away before we finished putting the place to flames. We ruined what there was of their fields and stores, but it looked as though they were ill-prepared for the winter."

Berkman shook his head slowly. "I cannot tell you true whether this were all just part of their deception, or if the village would have perished this winter even without our intercession."

He shrugged. "In the end, it matters not. The settlement is destroyed, and what captives we could take are taken from that place, and this band of savages will not harass our frontiers any longer."

As the man spoke, Joseph looked over the captives with frank curiosity. Other than the Oneida at Fort Sullivan, who were, during his brief time there, mostly kept separate from the massing force, and the brief look at the village to the north, he'd seen few Indians up close.

Though humbled and bound, the Iroquois did not avoid his eyes, and looked back at him with expressions that ranged from resignation and fear to outright hatred. As his gaze fell on one of the group, he thought he saw a brief start of recognition, but the warrior broke eye contact quickly and feigned boredom until Joseph had looked elsewhere.

Joseph was surprised to see a woman among their number, hardly more than a girl, he realized, with her hands tied before her and a look of confidence upon her face as she looked around at the other captives.

As Joseph was looking at her, the Lieutenant approached the group and spoke loudly to them. "Are there any among you who understand English?"

The warrior who'd attracted Joseph's attention looked up and said, in a heavily-accented and strangely soft-sounding voice, "I am speak the English."

"What is your name, English speaker?"

"I am name the Ginawo." To Joseph's ear, it sounded as though the warrior had said "kin at war," which he thought was an ominous name for a captive.

The Lieutenant, though, simply nodded. "What is your tribe, Ginawo?"

"We am Skarure, the gather-hemp." He appeared to give the Lieutenant a look of pleading as he added, "We not war at tribe you. Not war at any white tribe. Not want war any. We plant food ours, hunt the deer ours, not war."

The Lieutenant looked over to where Joseph sat, his arm

bandaged and bound against his chest in a sling. Pointing to the private, he said, "If you want no war, then why is he hurt, and his companion dead?"

He turned and spat, then asked, "Who is your chief?"

Ginawo's mouth set for a moment in an unreadable expression, then he answered, "Warrior kill the chief-elder. We have now no the chief. We am the farmer and the hunter and the woman. Warrior am fire the village. Skarure not live the winter."

A flash of anger in his eyes, Ginawo added, "We not fire at the village any white tribe. We not war any white tribe. White tribe war the Skarure why?"

The Lieutenant scowled deeply at the young warrior. "I have met few Indians who admitted their savagery against us, so your lies do not impress me."

He gestured over the heads of the captives, out to the distance, his voice rising as he spoke. "The Iroquois have burned and killed in our settlements, do you deny that? At Cherry Valley, your warriors scalped and killed women and children, and kidnapped dozens of innocents. My own cousin was taken, and I've heard naught of his fate, but must fear the worst for him."

Joseph saw understanding dawn in Ginawo's eyes as he listened to the Lieutenant's growing rage. One of the other captives spoke quickly to the young warrior, who nodded to him in reply.

"We not scalp the any. We farm the corn, we hunt the deer."

"And you shoot the scouts," the Lieutenant shouted, again pointing to where Joseph sat.

Howe stood up and approached the Lieutenant. Quietly, he said, "Did Sergeant Berkman bring back any of the weapons that the detachment found in the village?"

The Lieutenant looked around sharply at Howe. Without looking away, he called out, "Sergeant Berkman, did you seize weapons in the raid?"

Berkman replied, "Yes, sir, 'twere a few war-clubs, some knives and a couple of bows that we took."

Howe asked him, "Did you seize any arrows to accompany the bows?"

Berkman looked puzzled and answered slowly, "I busted off a few arrowheads to keep as mementos, but I did not bother with the arrows."

"May I see one of the arrowheads? I shall return it in a moment, I assure you."

Digging around in his satchel for a moment, Berkman produced the barbed flint arrowhead, which Howe examined for a moment, and then held up for the Lieutenant to see. Quietly, he said, "I do not mean to speak out of turn, but I think the warrior speaks the truth, Lieutenant. The arrow I pulled from Private Killeen's arm had no head, as I think I mentioned to you. It was likely some other tribe that attacked my men."

The Lieutenant looked at the arrowhead that Howe held up for a moment, and then turned back to the captives, his mouth set in a grim, tight line. "You still must answer for the deaths of my men at your village, Ginawo."

It was Ginawo's turn now to assume a grim expression for a moment before he replied. "We defend from your men the village, they put the fire to the home we. You defend the home you. Men kill the elder-chief, kill the warrior, take the people. We war to the men, yes, the men war to us."

The Lieutenant stood facing the young warrior for another moment, his jaw muscles working, and then answered, "The Iroquois Confederation joined with our enemies, the British King, and has conducted cruel warfare against our people. Do you deny that your tribe is Iroquois?"

"Skarure am Haudenosaunee, call Iroquois at you. We not war at tribe you, not Haudenosaunee all war at tribe you." Ginawo shrugged, his face sad. "All tribe you war at all tribe Haudenosaunee, all tribe Haudenosaunee war at all tribe you, all war all time all people. All kill, all die."

He shook his head, his shoulders slumping, sadness emanating from his whole posture. "No. No, no, no. All not war at all."

Ginawo turned away, and he spoke with his companions for a few moments, clearly giving them a summary of the discussion.

The Lieutenant stood by until Ginawo and his companions were finished conferring, and then quietly said to the warrior, "I will come and speak with you again after I have given my report to my chief."

Turning to Berkman before striding away, he snapped, "See to it that these prisoners have water and food."

Chapter 9

Ginawo stirred, the bindings about his wrists waking him and returning him to his nightmare. Nearby, in the dim light cast by his captors' banked fire, he could see Jiwaneh's form, sleeping as uncomfortably as he had been. He hoped that she was staying warm despite the chill in the air.

Beyond her, he could see Tanarou staring up at the night, his eyes glittering darkly as lay there, brooding. Quietly, Ginawo said, "What will they do with us, honored elder?"

After a long pause, the older man replied. "I do not know, Ginawo. Perhaps they will enslave us, or give us to the Algonquin to gain favor with their chiefs, or buy back their prisoners. It is possible that they will have their sport with us yet, to avenge an attack against their settlements."

Tanarou sighed. "I will confess to you that I was surprised that they took us as prisoners; I expected that they would either kill us all, or, if we were very fortunate, leave us in peace. I did not expect this, and with Nitchawake's wisdom now lost to us, it falls to me to think of what we ought to do."

A thought occurred to Ginawo. "Did you notice that the man that their elder thought we had attacked was one of the scouting party whom I said we ought to attack for the safety of the People?"

"Indeed, there were two of the three of that party present

today. The missing man must be the soldier whom they said was killed. It was curious indeed that they knew that the People had not harmed these men after they saw our arrowheads."

The older man thought for a moment, then mused, "They may have been ambushed by warriors from the Onondaga. As their land is not so rich with the right sort of stone, they are in the habit of using arrows of wood alone. Our clan-brothers in that tribe are driven by rage to do foolish things in these days, since the sacred flame of the Haudenosaunee was extinguished at their village this spring past."

Ginawo could just see Tanarou's head shake in sorrow. "We avenge, they avenge. As you said to them, if we all are at war with everyone, then surely we all shall die."

Ginawo rolled to face Tanarou in the darkness, and as he did so, he felt the bindings about his left ankle loosen. He froze, and then pulled his leg up experimentally to see whether he might be able to slip his foot through the loop.

Tanarou could hear him moving around, but could not make out what the younger man was up to. "What are you doing, Ginawo?"

Lowering his voice even more, Ginawo whispered, "I believe I may be able to free my feet. If I can, then perhaps I can escape."

"Can you free your hands? If you can, then perhaps you can release us all."

Ginawo pulled hard at the cords that bound his wrists, but all he succeeded in doing was to pull them tighter. "I cannot, honored elder."

He thought for a moment, even as his feet continued to worry at the bindings on his ankles. He stopped suddenly. "If I can escape, but cannot free you... or Jiwaneh... then what good does that do me? I will not leave you, and I will not leave her."

He could hear the older man sigh, and Tanarou answered, "As your elder, I would command you to leave me, if you could, but I will not command you to leave Jiwaneh. However, I do think that you should continue the attempt to free your feet, so that you can discover whether it is possible to release her, even with your hands bound."

Ginawo nodded, then realized that the other man could not see the gesture in the darkness. "I will continue to attempt to discover whether I can free myself."

As he pushed at the knot that sat on the knob of his ankle, his foot slipped, and his heel thumped to the ground, where it landed on a twig. The resulting crack felt to him as though it had been as loud as a gunshot, and he froze.

Indeed, the Colonial soldier responsible for guarding the captives in the night ambled over, carrying a torch in his hand. He wandered through the ranks of still forms arrayed about on the ground, but he could not discern which were sleeping, and which were merely feigning sleep.

When he walked away to return to the side of the fire, Ginawo resumed his slow struggle against the cords the bound his feet, until he finally had to succumb to sleep without any further pretense.

Chapter 10

"How is the arm this morning, Joseph?" Sitting on a rolled-up blanket, Howe chewed his hardtack energetically and cupped his hands around his tea, savoring the smell of the steam that rose from its surface in the crisp air at sunrise.

"About as you would expect, Sergeant," Joseph replied, gingerly lifting the wounded arm to gauge its soreness. "It should be right as ever it was, in time."

He smiled, adding, "I expect it will be something to show the girls back home when this is all over. My neighbor's daughter Hannah might be impressed."

Becoming more serious, he said, "I owe you a debt of gratitude, Sergeant. Without you had thought so clear as to abandon William, we would very likely have been all struck down in that spot, and I'd have aught to show anyone every again. I owe you my life, and that's a fact."

"It is but the duty that I owed you, Joseph, but I'm glad to have preserved you. I am grieved that we lost William, but there was no way for us to have known that an ambush awaited us."

He pursed his lips, adding, "Though it may be that we were followed from the village that we scouted for intelligence." Shaking his head to dispel the ghosts that lay heavily about at the early morning of the day, he said, "In the event, what's done is done, and we have but to consider what might be yet to come."

Joseph regarded the sergeant for a few moments. "You did right yesterday, showing the Lieutenant that our captives could not have been those who attacked me. That Indian gave a good account of himself, as well, though it were difficult to make out exactly what he meant at times."

Howe nodded. "That was one smart Indian. There's not much call for them to learn English, this far removed from the frontier, and yet he was able to give the Lieutenant a proper what-for, despite all of that."

Joseph asked, "What of the Indians? Will they be dispatched to Fort Sullivan, or will they find some other disposal?"

"In truth, I know not, Joseph. If that Ginawo is to be believed, they are as innocent as the Oneida of the attacks upon our settlements in these parts, which makes what was done to them yesterday a sad injustice."

Howe grimaced, and added, "However, 'tis also true that this band has proven themselves deceitful, with their attempt to make their village look less than it truly was, and their ambush of the detachment."

He shook his head. "If I were the General, I think that I might release them—after all, they will not pose any threat to the settlements in this area for some time to come, with their village put to the torch, their weapons seized, and their elders slain."

Joseph objected, "On the other hand, even if they were previously kindly disposed toward our cause, or at worst, desirous of staying neutral, we have now given them ample cause to seek revenge, have we not?"

Howe nodded. "It may be that theirs is an unjust fate, but

at this moment, it is not ours to weigh. I expect that we will receive direction from the Lieutenant soon enough, and then it will be not ours to weigh either."

Stuffing the last bit of his hardtack into his mouth, and following it with the bitter remnants of his tea, Howe stood. "Let us get you to the quartermaster and have him change your bandages, as he asked."

When the Lieutenant emerged from the command tent to speak with Berkman, he seemed considerably calmer than he had the previous afternoon.

"Sergeant, the general wants the prisoners transmitted for safekeeping to Fort Sullivan. I'll detail you and four others to escort them, and expect you to rejoin us with all possible haste. Have you any questions?"

"Nay, sir, I misdoubt that they'll present any difficulty. I'll need supplies, of course, to feed the lot of them as we go."

The Lieutenant waved his hand toward the quartermaster's wagon. "Speak to MacDonohugh, but remember that every bit you take for the savages is one less bit that we have for our own bellies."

"Aye, sir, I shall not forget it."

The Lieutenant nodded. "Very well. I want to see you headed south within the hour."

"Aye, sir." Berkman saluted clumsily and took his leave, gathering up the men he'd need and then heading toward the supply wagon, knowing that talking MacDonohugh into releasing what little was needed would probably be more difficult than the rest of the march ahead.

Chapter II

As usual, Tanarou was awake and alert long before Ginawo. Raising himself as best he could on one elbow with his wrists still bound, he saw that Jiwaneh stirred also. He guessed that she was probably warmer than he, as the Colonists had seen fit to supply her with a blanket, one of the very few that they had passed out.

The blanket fell away from her face and her eyes flew open. Tanarou watched her suffer a momentary attack of panic, until she remembered where she was and why her ankles and wrists were tied. As her face cast about wildly, she saw Ginawo slumbering beside her, and visibly calmed. Turning the other way, her eyes met Taranou's, and he gave her a wry, reassuring smile.

Speaking softly, so as to let Ginawo get what rest he could before the ordeals of the day began, he said, "Ginawo told me that you wanted to share his doom, whatever it might be." He shrugged at the girl. "So here you are. It's not as bad as it could have been, right?"

Fighting to calm her breath, Jiwaneh said to him, "I did not imagine that this would be our fate, and yet I cannot say that I regret at all sharing it with him."

She paused for a moment, and then asked, "What is our fate to be, honored elder?"

He shrugged again, his expression growing more serious.

"That I do not know, and the wisdom of the elders has not yet been granted to me, so I cannot see the what the future likely holds for us, either."

His gaze wandered over to where some of their captors were gathering, surrounding the leader of the group that had razed the village the previous day. "I suspect that we will shortly learn, however."

Gesturing with a toss of his nose toward Ginawo, he said, "You should wake him now; he will need a few minutes to be ready for whatever the pale men have in mind for us."

The girl looked over at the Colonials to see what Tanarou was talking about, and then wriggled her way over to Ginawo, where she spoke urgently and quietly into his ear.

His eyes opened and he looked at her for a moment, before saying, "You are the straight-limbed maiden I had dreamed of, and I sorrow that I cannot yet hold you in my arms."

Tanarou snorted and laughed, saying, "You ought be careful what you hope for from your dreams, my young friend, or else be more complete in the details of your wishes."

"I see that our revered elder is in his normal morning mood," Ginawo observed, pushing himself up on one elbow and then drawing his knees to his chest to raise himself to a sitting position.

He grunted with the effort and winced as he discovered a bruise on his thigh in the process. Whether from the fighting yesterday or a rock under the leaves upon which he'd slept, his leg was stiff and sore.

"I hope that your beds were more comfortable than mine," he said, stretching his legs and trying to reach the sore spot to massage it out.

Tanarou said, "Nowhere close to as comfortable as the graves in which I expected to slumber last night, but not so uncomfortable as our former beds which smolder even yet."

He drew in a deep breath and nodded. "Can you not smell our longhouses in the air this morning?" Indeed, a faint, sharp reek of burnt wood and the distinctive note of smoldering leather could be smelled on the breeze that flowed over their camp from the direction of the former location of their settlement.

Ginawo nodded, "As is your annoying morning habit, honored elder, you are right enough."

He looked at Jiwaneh and added, "I will find it more pleasant to not speak at all in the morning, until the dust of sleep has cleared from my eyes and the mist of dreams from my mind."

The girl laughed a tiny bit, which did both men's hearts good. Around them, the other captured warriors who had awoken looked over to see what had prompted the unexpected mirth in the midst of their predicament.

Also looking in some wonder at the sound was their chief captor, another who wore a blue ribbon in his hat. He strode over to where Ginawo sat, and said something to him, and the other captives looked expectantly to the gifted young warrior for a translation.

"We are to prepare ourselves to go," said Ginawo, after responding to the Colonial warrior in the guttural speech of their kind.

The Colonial held out his hand to assist Ginawo to his feet and made an additional comment, which Ginawo wryly translated, "And we are not to make any trouble, nor attempt escape."

He bent and offered his bound hands to Jiwaneh, pulling her upright, and then shuffled over to where Tanarou still lay to do likewise. The Colonial took note of his difficulty and barked out a few words to his men.

Four soldiers came over in response to his command, and began untying the ankles of each of the captives. With gestures and unintelligible words, they directed the captives to line up single-file, and then bound them, one to the next at a distance of the height of a man, in a line with a rope secured about the captives' waists and looped through their still-bound hands.

Ginawo had been placed at the head of the line, so that he could relay commands to the rest of the captives, and in the course of this process, he, Tanarou and Jiwaneh were separated, with four or five warriors lined up between them.

Seeing that there was little to be done about it, though, Ginawo tried to comfort Jiwaneh, saying, "They assure me that we are to be treated well, and that there is food enough for our journey."

"Journey to where?"

"They have not yet said where we are to go," he answered, "but they did say that it should be a march of not more than seven or eight days."

She nodded. "We are not to be given to the Algonquin, then?"

"You were awake while Tanarou and I talked last night?"

"Enough to hear your concerns," she answered. "I hope that we are not to be sport for the enemy. The Algonquin warriors are said to have a ravenous appetite for the flesh of young girls they have taken in war."

He smiled at her, saying, "I am sure that those are tales told by old women to keep girls from taking chances that could result in their capture. The Algonquin, though they be our enemies for as long as the tales can relate, are still but men like us, and I doubt that they are any more depraved in their appetites than are we."

Tanarou, from near the back of the line of captives, spoke up now. "You have not fought against them, Ginawo, as have I. They can, indeed, be fearsome, and I have seen for myself the evil things that they will do, if given the chance."

He took a deep breath, and, surprised at the tears that sprang to his eyes as he recalled his own loss, said, "They do indeed seize young girls in war and take them away, never to been seen again. I have seen that for myself, as well, and can attest to the malicious glee with which they commit such acts."

Then he sighed, admitting, "Of course, we will do evil things in our turn, as well. We do not like to admit it, but any time we permit ourselves to believe that our enemies are inherently different from ourselves, that they are not as human as we are, it becomes an easy matter to do inhuman things to them."

He gestured with his bound hands at the Colonials who moved among them, checking their knots and offering each of the captives a sip of water and a few bites of thin stew. He said, "We will do well to remember the humanity of our antagonists on this day, and hope that by doing so we can encourage them to view us as being no less human than they are."

Ginawo nodded, catching in turn the eyes of each of the other warriors bound in line between himself and his companion elder. "We shall endeavor to do so, and hope that it will be to our benefit."

With a shout, the leader of the group now urged his men and their captives into motion, marching away from the encampment, and out of reach of the smoke that Taranou's sharp sense of smell could still detect.

Chapter 12

Trudging down the track beside the bound Indians, Joseph was beginning to have second thoughts about having volunteered to accompany them back to Fort Sullivan. When he'd asked Sergeant Howe for his thoughts, the man had shrugged, saying "'Tis your choice, Joseph. Berkman's a good fellow to work with, and it will give your arm some more time to heal before you must take on heavier duties."

However, there had been supplies to carry, and he had not figured on how being around the captives would affect him. Of course, communication was limited to gestures, and what English Ginawo could speak, but the bearing of the captives was heartbreaking.

It was not difficult to see that these were people who were proud and strong when in their element, and that their losses of the previous days had been bewildering for them. For the most part, they maintained a stoic pose, but there were all too many moments where the mask slipped, and one or another of the captives would look sadly about the forests through which they passed, or take note with sorrowful eyes the flight of a passing songbird.

Watching them stumble as they walked, their customary grace impaired by their fetters, Joseph could but imagine what thoughts passed through their minds. If Ginawo's words were to be taken at face value, then this band truly were innocent bystanders, caught up in events from which they'd had every intention of remaining aloof.

Joseph approached Sergeant Berkman, jogging forward in the formation to catch up with him for a moment. "Sergeant, I wonder if I might have a word with the Indian Ginawo?"

Berkman grunted, saying, "Won't hardly do any harm, now, will it, and 'twill pass the time as we march."

"Thank you, sir. I will report if I learn anything of use."

"Very good, Private. Just don't hold us up none, is all I ask."

Joseph nodded, and stepped over to where Ginawo walked, at the head of the chain of bound-together captives.

"Ginawo?"

Joseph was surprised when the warrior turned to him and said, "Am know you," his expression unreadable.

"You... know me?"

Ginawo nodded slowly. "Am see you and warrior others, when wake you while walk."

Joseph puzzled over this statement and asked, "You saw me and William and Sergeant Howe? With the ribbon on his hat?" He motioned at his own hat to indicate what he referred to.

Ginawo nodded. "We am see you, three were you then. Two now." He bowed his head. "Am sorrow died friend you."

Joseph looked sharply at him. "Were you telling the truth, that you had nothing to do with his death, or my wound?" He motioned at his still-bandaged arm.

Ginawo gave him a somber look, answering, "We not war at you. We not attack at you. See at you, yes. I think war at you, yes. Not war at you, left safe you, tell see you at village us. Elders decide not war at you." He shrugged. "You war at us, you fire at home us."

Joseph pondered this for a moment absorbing the fact that this warrior had held his fate in his hand, and had left him and his companions unmolested. He thought about their mission, and was then moved to ask, "Were there no children in your village?"

"Child live at village, yes. You war at us, child with others go." Ginawo stopped speaking abruptly, and Joseph knew that he'd said more than he'd intended to.

The wind had shifted, now blowing cold out of the north, and the first few pellets of sleet began spitting through the gaps in the trees as they walked on and Joseph considered what Ginawo's words implied. Berkman's guess had been right, then, and the village had been evacuated prior to the raid.

"Are there many others from your village, then? Where have they gone?"

Ginawo regarded Joseph, as though taking his measure as a man, before answering, "Not say to you, tribe, family safe must."

Joseph nodded slowly. "I understand, and I do not fault you for refusing to tell me." Struck by a sudden desire to measure up to the warrior's unspoken standard, he added, "I would not tell you, either, were our positions reversed. I respect your care for your people."

Ginawo nodded. "Thank you. What am name to you?"

"I am Joseph, Joseph Killeen."

"Joseph." Ginawo nodded, the strange name unfamiliar to his mouth, sounding more like "jo-tep" as he said it. "We go at where?"

Joseph replied, after considering for a fraction of a second whether there were any imprudence in doing so, "We're to take you to Fort Sullivan; after that, I know not what is to be done with you."

Ginawo grimaced. "You we sell at Algonquin there."

Joseph was taken aback at the accusation, and replied, "Nay, we are not such monsters! We do not sell captives, though we may ask labor of you until you are to be paroled, such as will ensure that you are fed."

"What am 'parole?' No am know this word."

"Oh, you know, you give your word to no longer take any hostile acts, and we release you with the understanding that you may be imprisoned once again, should you take up arms against us or assist those who do."

"Then am parole we now."

Joseph was startled by this argument, but he could not answer it. He said, slowly, "I don't know whether our officers would accept your parole, but it cannot hurt to ask, I suppose." The fitful bursts of sleet had become a steady downpour, the tiny pellets of ice making a high-pitched tone as they struck the leaves and trees the group passed through.

"Are your people warm enough?" Joseph's concern was genuine, but so was his desire to move on to a less uncomfortable topic.

Ginawo shrugged. "Am live at cold many winter." He appeared to struggle with how to say what he wanted to add to this, and finally settled for, "Am stay at longhouse we at winter, not walk at snow."

He gave Joseph what could only be described as a reproachful look, and then glanced upward at the sky. "Snow fall at us soon, much. Not am warm enough then."

Just then, Joseph heard Berkman call out, "We will stop for lunch now, men. Private Hardy, get a fire going, that we may have some warmth against this miserable weather."

Hardy replied, "Yes, sir," and immediately began ranging about to collect firewood, as the rest of the group gratefully came to a halt, their captives motioned into a circle, where they huddled together for warmth.

"I've a tinderbox, if you need," Joseph volunteered, but the other man shook his head in reply.

"Nay, I've my own, but thank ye kindly. Save yours for when you've again got the task."

"Private Killeen, could I speak with you, please?" Berkman looked weary and irritable, his collar pulled tight up on his neck, and his hat low over his face.

"Certainly, sir." Joseph hurried over.

"Did you learn anything of interest in your conversation with the savage?"

"Aye, sir. I learned that they do not ordinarily range out in weather such as this, and that they would prefer to be close to hearth and home." He shrugged. "I think that they do not resent us for making them travel in the cold, but it would be a kindness to get them to the fort as quickly as possible."

Nodding toward the group of miserable-looking Indians, he added, "The warrior Ginawo wondered, too, whether they could offer parole, as they have no interest in fighting against us. I told him that would be a matter for the officers to decide," he added hastily.

"Indeed it shall, Killeen, and I've no doubt that our officers will refuse parole to savages who've already proven their skill at deception."

He frowned. "They're not to be trusted, Private, and don't you forget that. I buried two men at that damned village, men with families and futures. They died because these savages ignore all civilized standards of warfare, and do not acknowledge with proper humility when a superior force has bested them."

Joseph frowned in turn. "They were but defending their homes, Sergeant, and you heard Ginawo say yesterday that they were not desirous of war with us at all."

Berkman motioned impatiently with his hand. "Words, Private, just words." A gust of wind filled his face with sleet and he scowled. "This storm is shaping up to be a great hindrance to our journey. Go and help Hardy gather wood for a fire, at least."

By the time the fire was started, the sleet had shifted by imperceptible degrees into snow, wet and heavy, which began to lay about in short order, making the ground slippery and wet as the men moved about, preparing tea and gnawing at dried beef.

With a look of deep disgust, Sergeant Berkman finally ordered the men to make camp for the day. As they did so, the snow continued to fall, although, mercifully, the wind lessened.

Ginawo spoke up, "We am build longhouse for warm, help." He gestured at the tarpaulins the men were unfolding in preparation for setting up their tents.

Looking even more disgusted, Berkman said, "We'd best get their help. Hillson, unbind their hands, but hobble them with cords about their ankles, and perhaps three or four feet of cord between, that they cannot run."

The private jumped to the task, and Joseph moved to help.

"Nay, Killeen, you attend to the fire, and permit Hardy to bind the prisoners."

Joseph nodded, wondering whether Berkman considered him suspect for having conversed with Ginawo. For his part, Ginawo gave Joseph a quick smile as he helped the other men raise the large lean-to under which they all would take shelter.

By the time they had finished, the snow had switched back to sleet, then to a cold, heavy rain and the breeze had shifted to come out of the south. It was still biting and miserable, but it didn't seem to be getting any colder.

As the soldiers and their captives gathered under the lean-to, Joseph heard Hillson laughing crudely as he gestured at the girl among the captives, talking to his particular friend, Greene. His leer left little to the imagination as to what the comment had been about, and Joseph was aware of a sudden tension in Ginawo's bearing as he, too, caught the gist of the comment.

"They are prisoners, not playthings, Hillson," he said, flushing as all three privates turned to face him.

Greene called out, his tone taunting and rude, "What's it to you, Killeen? Did not one of the savages in these parts put a hole in your own arm?"

"Aye, but none of these prisoners had a part in that; just as we differ between British and American, they differ from tribe to tribe."

Sergeant Berkman spoke up now, saying, "Just as these States stand together, though they be independent entities, these Iroquois are all of one confederation, Private Killeen, and must all bear guilt for the attacks on our settlements and forces in these parts. That is why General Washington dispatched our forces here."

Turning to Greene and Hillson, he said, "We'll not be abusing our prisoners, however. The girl is to be delivered to Fort Sullivan unmolested, and the warriors unhurt. I have had very clear orders from the Lieutenant on this point exactly, and any who transgress are to be dealt with summarily."

The two privates shrank under Berkman's glare, but once the man had turned back to regard the prisoners, huddled together at the far side of the lean-to, both men gave Joseph looks that portended trouble for the wounded private.

The next morning, all three of the other privates seemed to be deaf to Joseph's presence any time that the sergeant was not around, but Joseph ignored their slights as the group worked together to tear down the campsite and prepare to resume their march southward in the cold, steady rain.

As they folded a tarpaulin together, Hardy hissed to Joseph, "You should consider carefully which side of this conflict you are on, Killeen. Is it true that your companion gathered a dozen arrows to the back while you took but one in the arm, so that you could escape suspicion?"

Joseph gaped at the man, who had until now been a relatively friendly fellow traveler. "Have you taken leave of your senses, Hardy? I am no friend to those who killed my companion William, and I take offense extremely at your suggestion. Are you and your fellows so desperate for the illicit abuse of a prisoner that you would accuse me outright of sympathizing with our enemies?"

"You seem to know not who your enemies are, Killeen." With that, the other man took the folded tarpaulin roughly out of his hands and shoved past him, deliberately running his elbow into Joseph's wounded arm.

Joseph cried out in pain and clutched at the wound, which throbbed at the fresh insult.

"Mind your step better, Private Killeen," Berkman called out. "We haven't time to stop and physic you if you should re-open your wounds."

Burning with anger at his fellow soldiers, Joseph kept his distance from them for the remainder of the process of preparing for the day's march. As they formed up to depart, Berkman summoned him to his side. "I'll have your company with me as we march today, Private, if you don't mind. The savages have had quite enough conversation for the moment."

Joseph withheld comment, but acquiesced, taking his place at the sergeant's side as they marched onward into the forest.

Chapter 13

Ginawo, although he was accustomed to making long treks alongside Tanarou, was weary and footsore. His discomfort was increased by the awareness that behind him in the line, Jiwaneh was suffering far worse than he. It wasn't helped, either, by his growing concern about her safety in the company of the Colonial soldiers.

Ginawo was gratified that Joseph had spoken in her defense, but he could see that it had cost the young soldier dearly. He had watched, silent, as Joseph had endured the cold glares and outright abuse of his fellows, and he regretted that the man seemed to be paying the price for doing what should have been Ginawo's to do, himself.

He heard one of the warriors cry out from behind him, and he was jerked to a stop by the cord about his waist. Turning, he saw that Ohakeh had fallen, and Jiwaneh was bent beside him, trying to help him back to his feet. The warrior lay still on the muddy track, and a chill ran down Ginawo's spine as he realized that another of his tribe was gone.

He exchanged a look with Tanarou, who looked on as helplessly as Ginawo himself felt, while Jiwaneh struggled fruitlessly to rouse the dead man.

She pulled at his hands, tears running down her face. "His spirit has gone, Jiwaneh," Tanarou said quietly from behind her.

She turned, crying, "For what reason? He was healthy, strong and unhurt. I do not understand."

He shrugged, his expression sad but composed. "He gave up, Jiwaneh. Some spirits cannot tolerate being in captivity, and depart rather than remain in bonds."

She turned away from Tanarou and sought comfort in Ginawo's eyes. He wished that he could hold her and tell her that all would be as it ought, but she was denied even that comfort by the cords that held them still in place.

The soldiers gathered about the stricken man, satisfying themselves that he was, in fact, expired, and then, at their chief's impatient commands, untied the corpse and dragged it off the track, unceremoniously dumping Ohakeh in the forest. Ginawo felt a resurgence of his grief over the missed drums, singing and remembrance that should have been Ohakeh's, as well as that of the others who had been lost to the village in the past days.

As the soldiers adjusted the cords between their prisoners, he heard the sound of a scuffle, and then one of the soldiers cursed and, turning to the noise, Ginawo saw him strike Jiwaneh full across the face with his open hand.

What happened next was too fast for Ginawo to fully grasp until it was all over. Both he and Tanarou lunged toward where Jiwaneh stood, her hand rising to her reddened face. The rest of the warriors likewise rushed the soldiers who had been around the girl.

Tangled in the lines that bound their captives together, two of the Colonials tripped and fell into the mud, but the one who had struck Jiwaneh kept his footing until Ginawo tackled him.

Even as he held down Jiwaneh's assailant, the one called

Greene, Ginawo could hear the chief's hoarse shout of surprise behind him. Grasping Greene's head and twisting it sharply, Ginawo felt the soldier's death-shudder under him.

Beside him, he could see the one called Hardy turning purple as one of the warriors throttled him with the cord that bound him to the next warrior. Tanarou had found a rock and was using it to dispatch Hillson.

Behind him, Ginawo heard another warrior cry out, and turned to see that the Colonial's chief had plunged a knife into Rawanake's back. However, he was unable to pull it free before the brothers Itararo and Hatopeh, working together as always, overpowered him, simply pushing his face into the mud and holding him there until the soldier's thrashing ceased.

Standing off at a distance, where the sergeant had dispatched him to conceal Ohake's corpse while the other men re-tied their captives, Joseph wore an expression of shock and terror as the band of prisoners turned from their grisly work to look at him.

"No," said Ginawo. "I will speak with him."

Chapter 14

His hands still shaking despite the cord that bound them before him, Joseph walked between Ginawo in front of him, and a tall older warrior introduced to him as Tanarou behind him. The shocking suddenness of the change in his circumstances was beginning to catch up with him.

When Ginawo had approached him, carrying a knife taken from Greene's belt, Joseph had been certain that he was going to quickly join his erstwhile companions in their eternal slumber.

However, Ginawo had stopped before him, and looked him in the eyes, saying, "You help at we." Pointing at where the girl stood, still bearing a bright red handprint on her cheek, he continued, "You safe him."

Nodding to his companions, he said, "You walk with we, not war at you."

Joseph, looking at the band of Indians as they busied themselves with knives at the corpses of their defeated enemies, couldn't restrain himself and said, "For a people who do not wish to practice the arts of war, you are all too effective at them."

Ginawo turned to look and turned back to regard Joseph. "The soldier make bad at him Jiwaneh, we make war at the soldiers. We am not want make war at soldiers, not want make war at you."

Joseph returned Ginawo's gaze. "What will you do with

me?"

Ginawo shrugged. "Elders decide at you. We bring you at elders now." With a toss of his head, he motioned for Joseph to follow him. After brief consideration, Joseph sighed and followed the man.

Ginawo had exchanged words with his companions as they cleaned their knives and put away the trophies they had collected from their vanquished foes. Evidently, there was some argument about Joseph's status among them, but in the end, Ginawo had approached him with a length of cord, saying, "Am sorry at you, must tie at the hands you. Chief you not parole we, we not parole you."

Nodding with resignation, Joseph placed his wrists before him and offered no resistance as the Indian tied them. Ginawo tied them with hands that were gentle, but Joseph knew that behind that gentleness was a steel will.

Their pace back toward the former site of his captor's village was considerably faster than it had been on the journey south, but he could tell that some of the warriors ached to rid themselves of the impediment that his presence represented. The brothers—they appeared to Joseph to be twins—kept ranging far ahead of the group, and then loping back.

More than once, Joseph saw them fingering the blades they'd liberated from the corpses of the Colonial soldiers as they looked at him, though they ceased menacing him outright this way on a sharp word from Tanarou.

Joseph was struck by how quiet the party was, despite their speed. As they came over a small rise, a deer, so close that the brothers nearly collided with it, startled at the sight of them and bounded away, white tail flashing a warning to its fellows.

Joseph had never seen a live deer at such close range before, and knew that a typical party of Colonials would have frightened it off long before they'd gotten so close. While the brothers followed the animal with their eyes as it crashed through the undergrowth, Joseph simply stared in wonder.

Ginawo turned and grinned at him. "Brothers am wish have arrow at him, feed all." He shrugged and they set off again.

The rain had stopped shortly after the defeat of the Colonial squad, and as the afternoon sun began to dim into evening grey, Tanarou called a halt. The Indians, using the supplies they'd seized from their former captors, set up their campsite quickly and efficiently.

Joseph longed for some hot tea, but one of his captors had tossed aside the brick of tea after gnawing on a corner of it. Ginawo offered him a mouthful of water and a bit of hardtack, and he had to satisfy himself with that. The Indians saved the jerky for themselves, not without some exaggerated chewing from the brothers, in particular.

Settling down to sleep, he heard Ginawo and the girl speaking in hushed, tender tones, and Joseph nodded to himself. He had done the right thing in upbraiding his fellow soldiers for their treatment of the young woman, though he could not have guessed that this act would swiftly save his life. For the moment, at least— the morrow, and the elders, might bring a different conclusion.

Chapter 15

H olding Jiwaneh gently in his arms as the first rays of the morning sun slanted into his eyes, Ginawo pondered the whirlwind of events that had taken place over the course of mere days. He had no home now, but he had a wife. He had been free, captive and now captor. He had lost five of his tribe mates, and had taken a life with his own hands.

Jiwaneh stirred, and started, then relaxed as she fully realized where she was. Turning to face Ginawo, she said, "I awake as from a dream, and yet you are no dream, but real and here."

Ginawo smiled at her and said, "I am no dream, it is true. If I were a dream, I would not need so badly to find a bush." She laughed and disentangled herself from his arms. On his way back to the campsite, he noted that most of the rest of his group were awake, some more alert than others. Joseph sat quietly, staring into space, on one side of the camp, while the brothers Itararo and Hatopeh conversed amongst themselves.

Crouching beside the brothers, Ginawo said, "This captive of ours kept Jiwaneh from suffering a greater insult than she did. It is for the elders to decide, but I would see him adopted into the Bear Clan, to take the place of those we have lost."

The brothers looked at him, their expressions inscrutable, then Itararo said, "If that is the decision of the elders, then we will welcome him to the tribe. Hatopeh and I will give him no further trouble before the elders have spoken."

Ginawo nodded, grateful. "I cannot ask more than that."

Continuing over to where Joseph sat, he checked on the cord that bound the soldier's wrists together, ensuring that they were not cutting into his flesh. Standing, he gave Joseph a quick smile, hoping to give him strength and courage for a difficult day of travel.

Ginawo knew that the knots were more symbolic than anything else—Joseph could certainly run even with his hands bound—and he saw no need for unnecessary injury to a man whom he might soon call brother.

He walked to Taranou's side. The older man turned and grunted. "I am surprised at seeing you up and moving about with no prompting from me for once."

Ginawo smiled at him, replying, "Honored elder, I would slumber yet, had I not drunk so deeply of the brook last night."

Tanarou laughed, and Ginawo said, "I would speak with you, if I may, honored elder."

"Of course, Ginawo. What is in your mind?"

"I have thought about this soldier, and that he did what was right, at the cost of provoking his fellow pale men to set him apart from their company. And I have spoken with him at length. I would like to ask the elders to permit his adoption into the Bear Clan."

Tanarou raised his eyebrows, but said nothing for some time, as he let the thought run about in his mind, considering the many ramifications that it would have. He looked over at the Colonial, sitting yet, still and quiet, awaiting his doom.

Slowly, he nodded. "I can see the good in that." Looking at

the younger man, and seeming to take his measure afresh, he added, "You are gaining in wisdom, Ginawo, and you have led your people with some very creative decisions already. I suspect that the elders will see the strength of your idea, as well."

He shrugged. "Or they may see to exchange him for prisoners taken from the People, or decide that he poses too great a threat to our safety if he remains alive. Let us find the People and relieve his worry."

Ginawo nodded, replying, "Thank you, revered elder. As always, I value your point of view. I will get the camp cleared so that we be on our way."

After the dreary cold rain of the prior day, the sunshine made for pleasant travel. As the sun warmed them, everyone in the party seemed to feel more energetic, and they made good time through the forest.

In addition to being in a somber mood, though, it was apparent that Joseph was in increasing pain from the wound on his arm. Throughout the day, Ginawo noticed that the soldier was holding the arm close by his side as he walked, and once, when he bumped into a tree on the injured side, he cried out aloud.

When they stopped to rest, he called Jiwaneh over to where Joseph sat, his face grey and haggard. "Will you look at his arm, and see if there is nothing we can do to make him more comfortable for the remainder of our journey?"

"I will do what I can, but I am no Karowenna."

"I know that you lack her years, Jiwaneh, but I have faith in your knowledge, nonetheless."

She smiled at Ginawo, and then, with gentle fingers, pulled the soldier's shirt to one side, exposing the bandage. She scowled in disapproval at the dirty rags, clotted with dried blood. Feeling the skin of his upper arm and shoulder, she shook her head and frowned with further concern.

Glancing about at the forest surrounding them, she pointed to a magnificent tree not far distant. "Bring me bark from under the skin of branches that have fallen from that one. And bring leaves from that one," she continued, indicating a birch just past it. "I need water, warmed over a fire, if we can."

Ginawo nodded wordlessly and motioned for three of the warriors to busy themselves with doing as she asked. He watched as she murmured reassurance to the injured man, and carefully undid the knots holding the filthy bandage in place. Once it was loosened, she lifted it away from his skin until she reached resistance, and then sat back on her heels to wait for the water to be ready.

Though she knew that he could not understand her words, she told Joseph, "You have a heat in your arm, but we can cool it. First, though, we must get rid of these foul bandages and give you something to drink that will help reduce the pain and heat."

Turning to Ginawo, she asked, "Can we remove his bindings, so that I can move his arm freely?"

"I can see no harm in that," he said, and bent to untie cords around Joseph's wrists.

The soldier winced as Jiwaneh now lifted his wounded arm, and she again smiled quickly and spoke soothingly to him, saying, "I do not mean to hurt you, but only to make this better." She looked over her shoulder and saw that two of the warriors Ginawo had dispatched were carefully gathering what she needed, while a third was feeding a small fire, a small pot—one they had recovered from the packs carried by the Colonials—full of water beside him.

After a short wait, during which Jiwaneh continued to speak quietly to Joseph, the warrior approached with the pot, saying, "The warm water you asked for, Jiwaneh. The brothers will be here shortly with the materials you had asked for."

She nodded gravely to him, saying, "Thank you. You may want to keep your distance now; this is going to hurt him. See if you can find me something that will serve to hold a poultice."

Ginawo stepped back a bit, but stayed close enough to offer Joseph comfort by holding the soldier's gaze with his own, and to translate, if necessary. Jiwaneh pulled Joseph's shirt all the way off his arm, to keep it dry while she worked. The soldier shivered slightly as the cold air struck his bare skin, but he did not voice any complaint.

The warrior who brought the water thought for a moment and returned in a moment with a strip of coarse cloth torn from a shirt he found in one of the knapsacks. Jiwaneh said, "Thank you, Mehwaro," though she did not look away from her hands, already busy pouring the warm water from the pot onto the bandage.

As it softened and cleared away some of the blood that was adhering the cloth to his skin, she began slowly easing it off Joseph's arm. The soldier was doing his best to be stoic, but whimpered aloud as she tugged at the part that was stuck to the wound itself.

With a sudden jerk, the bandage finally lifted free, and Jinaweh turned and dropped it directly into the small fire Mehwaro had built, where it hissed like a thing malevolently alive. She examined his arm, making small, disapproving noises in the back of her throat as she beheld the swelling around the wound, and the angry red streak up his arm.

"It would be best to have Karowenna look at this when we

rejoin the people of the village. However, I know that we had to leave much of her supplies behind when we left, so she, too, may no longer have what she needs to remove the excess fire from his arm."

Pointing at the redness that surrounded the wound and radiated up toward his shoulder, she said, "Here is too much fire, more even than the poultice and drink can remove. The poultice I will put on him will aid the wound in its healing, and the drink will douse some of the fire, and help him to feel less pain, but that alone will not likely put out this fire."

The girl grimaced. "The only other thing that I know to do is to douse it with cold water, until Karowenna can advise me to do something better."

Ginawo nodded at Mehwaro, who stood and ran off to get fresh water. Ginawo then said a few words to Joseph in the tongue of the pale men. He was doing his best to avoid looking at the wound, clearly unsettled at the sight of his damaged and infected arm, but he nodded in understanding.

The brothers brought back the bark and leaves Jiwaneh had demanded, and she immediately crumpled the leaves Itararo gave her and dropped them into the remaining water in the pot, but set aside the bark that Hatopeh handed her.

While she was doing her best to be brisk and to project confidence, the girl was shaken by the appearance of the soldier's arm. Only once had she seen even Karowenna treat a wound with so much flame within it, and that warrior, wounded in the pursuit of a stag, had taken many long days to recover. Indeed, his leg had never been as strong afterward, and the scar had been as awful to behold as the charred skin of a lightning-struck tree.

Mehwaro brought cold water back from the stream, and Jiwaneh said, "Now hold him down; this will hurt him nearly as much as would a scalping." Ginawo gave Joseph a piece of wood to bite onto, and explained to him what was coming. The soldier paled and nodded, putting the wood between his teeth and holding out his arms for the warriors to pin down.

Sucking an anticipatory breath in through her teeth, the girl, poured a bit of the water onto the wound, and then reached in to squeeze as much of the flame out of the soldier's flesh as she could. He tensed and bit down hard on the wood in his mouth, but remained silent, though tears trickled down his cheeks. She repeated the process three times more, until nothing but clear water issued forth from his injury.

She gently reached over and lifted the wood from his mouth, saying in a soothing tone, "The worst is over now. I have only to prepare the poultice and apply it." Ginawo translated briefly, and Joseph nodded, his skin still pale, and beads of sweat visible on his forehead.

Saying, "I ought to be doing this using medicine stones, but this must suffice," she stripped away the inner bark from the pieces that Hatopeh had brought her. Once she had the pale inner skin free of the woody outer parts that had clung to it, she put it into her mouth to chew it up, as Karowenna had taught her to do, if the stones were not available to grind with.

Taking a few leaves out of the water and adding them to the mash, she chewed for a moment, and then transferred the poultice to the cloth. After patting Joseph comfortingly on the back, she applied it to the wound, wrapped the cloth around his arm, and tied it securely. She then smiled reassuringly to him and pulled his shirt sleeve back up over his hand and arm, quickly retying the lacing in the front for him.

She then raised the pot of warm, infused water to his mouth and tipped it up for him to drink it. He made a face as he tasted the bitter concoction, but he drank anyway. When he was done, Joseph wiped his mouth on the sleeve of his unhurt arm.

The man took a deep breath and said a few words in his guttural tongue to Ginawo, who translated for him, "He gives his thanks, though he wishes that it had not hurt so badly."

Jiwaneh dipped her head to the soldier, saying, "I, too, wish it had not caused him so much pain. I hope that what I've done will enable us to quickly get him to Karowenna, who is the only person I know who can hope to fully quench the fire within his arm."

As the group got underway, though, it seemed as though her work on the soldier's wound had yielded dramatic results for him. As Ginawo had not seen fit to retie their prisoner's hands, after the first hour or so of walking, Joseph had begun moving the arm freely, and his color was greatly improved.

When the band stopped to eat, Jiwaneh examined the soldier's arm, nodding in approval as she noted that the swelling seemed to have reduced, and while the streak of inner flame was still visible on his skin, it was no worse, at least.

By the late afternoon, Tanarou was seeing familiar landmarks in the forest: the peculiar set of three granite boulders set into the side of a hill, a twisted old oak, its rust-colored leaves almost all stripped away by the wind, a wide stream with two trees fallen across it forming a handy footbridge. The people of the village would be nearby, but he was not certain where they might have fled to.

If the Colonial army had moved on, the elders would have taken shelter relatively nearby. However, if they had feared pursuit by the pale men, the elders would have driven the People to continue fleeing for as far as they were able.

As though he were able to hear the older man's thoughts, Ginawo strode up beside him and asked, "Honored elder, how far do you think that the people of the village travelled from this place?"

Tanarou answered, wryly, "I have been pondering that very question myself, Ginawo. Perhaps Joseph can tell us whether the pale men would have pursued the People, whether they even perceived that the People had fled, or if they would have been content to merely destroy our homes?"

Ginawo nodded, and dropped back to confer briefly with the captive soldier. Returning to Taranou's side, he reported, "He believes that the army's orders are to destroy villages, take what captives they can, and keep moving. They were aware of our ruse at the village; indeed, they believe that we were trying to create an ambush, like a hunter placing bait to attract the bear."

Ginawo paused for a moment, considering whether to continue, but plunged on, saying, "He did not believe that they would have dedicated the warriors needed to pursue and take our people, as the loss of the village was perceived to have been enough to prevent us from being any sort of threat to the Colonial warriors and settlers in the area."

Taranou's expression was grim as he replied, "There is no doubt about that—as a matter of fact, I am concerned about our ability to survive the winter with our longhouses in ashes, and an army about that might burn us out again at any time."

After a few moments' sour thoughts, though, he nodded. "At this moment, however, the question of how far away the elders would have felt the need to lead the People is probably answered as 'just out of reach.'"

Gesturing to the east, he said, "We will continue, then, until we reach the River of the Dancing Waters, and follow that for the rest of the day. If we have not yet found the People by the time we must make camp for the night, we will resume our search in the morning."

He uttered a sharp bark of laughter. "I do not think that any of us expected to have this problem. The elders were convinced that we would be killed, and we believed that we would either preserve the village for their return, or die. In any case, we never discussed with them how we might rejoin them after losing the village."

Ginawo smiled, perhaps for the first time since he had watched the flames leap up through the longhouses. "It is a good difficulty to face, respected elder."

Chapter 16

With the screaming throb of pain in his arm reduced to a dull, bearable ache, Joseph was able to give his situation more thought, even as he followed the band of Indians to whatever fate awaited him.

He did not think it likely that, after Jiwaneh had put so much effort into physicking his arm, the elders would decide to have him killed to further avenge the losses that the village had suffered, but he could not disregard the possibility that he might be spending his final hours on Earth walking in the forest.

The air had warmed considerably, and with the rays of the afternoon sun slanting over his shoulder through the now largely denuded trees, the light was gorgeous. As it darted amongst the branches, bits of sunlight highlighted spots of beauty that Joseph might otherwise have missed.

Like a living being, the sunlight showed him a squirrel, frozen in place for an instant before it chittered a scold at the passing humans, its tail twitching in irritation. It fell next on a cleft boulder, looking as though it had been dropped from far above by some playful giant. The intricately-wound branches of a yew bramble appeared in the next dapple, and then the shining white bark of a copse of birch.

The warmth of the autumn sun seemed to be waking a range of scents from the forest, as well. The sharp, agreeable aroma of a recently-snapped cedar trunk competed with the warm richness of the soil disturbed where it had fallen. As they passed beyond that, Joseph caught the musky, bitter echo of a skunk's standoff with some predator, and the gentler smell of the fallen leaves underfoot, just starting to molder in the damp from the recent rains.

He noticed that Tanarou was looking even more alert that usual, his nostrils flared, and an inscrutable expression on his face. A moment later, he detected a whiff of what must have grabbed the Indian's attention—a lingering scent of smoke in the air. With a palpable shock, he realized that it must be coming from the ruins of their village.

Joseph wasn't surprised when the Indians exchanged a few fluid-sounding words and pointed slightly to the north of their present course. Ginawo asked Tanarou something, and Tanarou answered briefly, nodding grimly. Ginawo turned northward then, and the rest of the party followed him, their mood becoming increasingly tense as they went.

Within a few more minutes of long, determined strides, the group came over a slight rise to behold the outer edges of a wide clearing in the forest. The smell of wet ashes lay heavily in the air, and Ginawo motioned for everyone to stay concealed while he ranged ahead, silent and cautious.

After several quiet minutes, which the Indians passed whispering among themselves, Ginawo returned and made a very brief declaration. His tribe mates stood as a group, and Joseph followed their example. Slowly, somberly, they filed out of the forest and into the clearing where once they had lived.

The first thing Joseph could see was a small field of corn, the stalks trampled flat and what ears remained torn from their husks and scattered in the dirt. A few smashed squash littered the ground, the shattered flesh already beginning to grow a layer of splotchy black mold.

Past the destroyed garden plot, the still-smoking beams of a longhouse stood, half collapsed, looking like the kicked-in ribs of some improbable beast—and one that had met a bitter end. One of the twins darted forward to retrieve a small carving, battered and blackened, from the ground at the entrance to the longhouse.

His expression was reflective of a brief moment joy at his discovery, set in the deep sadness at the destruction that lay thick about them. He brought the carving over to his brother, and the two of them ran their hands over it, blackening their fingertips with soot.

The other longhouses were in even worse condition. For the most part, they were utterly reduced to ash, with nothing retrievable from the wreckage. Joseph's captors appeared to be dazed by the devastation, and he was the recipient of not a few glares and muttered imprecations as they walked about their former homes.

Even Ginawo approached Joseph, saying with great emotion, "You see at village! Soldiers kill all, fire at all, am nothing at us now."

He motioned around at the desolation within the clearing, continuing, "Snow come, no longhouse, no food." He shook his head angrily and stalked off, taking up a stick with which he stirred the ashes of the longhouse that had stood in the center of the village.

Joseph had no inclination to answer, even if Ginawo's angry outburst had given him the opportunity to do so. He knew from the word around the Colonies that the Iroquois had been equally vicious, if not far more barbaric, in their attacks on settlements here in New York. The newspapers had been full of lurid stories of scalpings and kidnappings, and the sentiment among Joseph's neighbors had been strongly in favor of taking some action.

However, looking around at what remained of the village of the Skarure, and reflecting on Ginawo's words to the Lieutenant, Joseph was hard-pressed to say that this seemed like a response that was likely to result in peace in the long term. The survivors of this attack would have a desire for revenge, and the cycle of back-and-forth strikes seemed destined to continue forever, unless one or the other of the contestants were to eliminate each other entirely.

He raised his eyes from the ground to find Tanarou standing close by him, observing him minutely. The old Indian did not betray any emotion in his face, but his bearing was that of a judge, and Joseph found that he could not meet his eyes for very long without feeling the overpowering urge to look away.

He turned his gaze about the heaped rubble and ash, his expression sorrowful and his heart pressed tight within his chest. Just then, his ruminations were interrupted as a wail went up from Jiwaneh, at the far end of the village clearing.

Tanarou took Joseph's arm and led him toward where the girl was. The other Indians, too, gathered where she crouched, rocking on her heels and keening in sorrow. Before her lay a heap of skins, with a small arm protruding from beneath them.

Taranou's eyes narrowed as he knelt beside the girl, lifting the edge of the leather to behold what lay beneath. At the sight, he closed his eyes in pain and sat back on his heels, his hand coming to rest on Jiwaneh's shoulder in a gesture of comfort. He said a word or two to the other Indians, and his eyes brightened with tears as they muttered among themselves.

Ginawo knelt at Jiwaneh's other side, pulling the girl into his arms. Together they rocked for a long while, she weeping, and he looking fiercely into the distance. Eventually, he turned and uttered a brief command to the other Indians, and pulled Jiwaneh upright with him as he stood.

His voice bitter, he spoke to Joseph, his tongue rebelling against the English pronunciation. "Him am elder-mother village us, am call Karowenna. Soldier you shoot at him back, him run." At this, Ginawo's voice failed him and he turned away.

Joseph's cheeks burned with shame by association at the act of shooting an old woman in the back as she fled. The hope he had felt at the careful ministrations of the tribe members to his wound faded away as he looked down at the crumpled heap that had been an honored elder of the tribe.

Whatever charitable feelings might have been built up toward him as he conversed with Ginawo and was cared for by Jiwaneh had evaporated, and he knew that with one of their number so senselessly killed by his fellow soldiers, the tribe's elders would be ill-disposed toward him. His future, which had been murky before, now appeared dark indeed.

Chapter 17

After attending to the minimum of ceremonies necessary to ease Karowenna's formidable spirit in its passage to the next world, there being no drums left, and the rest of the elders somewhere in the forests, Tanarou turned his back on the ravaged village and led his small party away.

Ginawo took bitter comfort in the thought that if their captive's arm worsened, the only person who might have had the skill to attend to it lay dead behind them. Joseph's fate was no longer something that he or his companions had any influence over.

For her part, Jiwaneh was fierce in her determination to have nothing further to do with Joseph's recovery. "How can I use the knowledge given to me by Karowenna to bring comfort and health to the tribe mate of those who took her life?" Ginawo had no answer for her, and was not moved to urge her to reconsider.

The group trudged on into the east, the sun now low behind them, and Ginawo finally called them to a halt for the night. None seemed to have any will to hurry forward, and indeed, they barely had the energy or interest to even prepare food or shelter for the night.

They attended to these needs of the living out of a sense of duty, with the weight of the dead village and its dead matriarch lying heavily upon their souls. As they arrayed themselves upon the ground before the fire, Ginawo approached Joseph, and without a word, bound his wrists and ankles for the night.

Joseph lay awake as the sky darkened, looking at the implacable stars that gleamed through the bare branches overhead. He was unwilling to surrender to sleep, so concerned was he that he would be held to account for the deeds of his countrymen. He wondered if he would see the sun set another time, if this were the last time he'd pick out the familiar pattern of the Great Square, or await the rising of the Plough.

Just overhead, he could see the Cross, and thought about the experience of others who'd known, or guessed, that they might be lying down for their last rest before the final sleep of death took them. He wondered what a condemned man did to order his thoughts as he waited for his sentence to be carried out, and whether it was possible to find peace in the dark hours of a waning life.

Consumed with these black thoughts, Joseph slipped away lightly into sleep, waking only when Ginawo's infamous snoring became so loud that even Jiwaneh had to poke the young warrior in the ribs and get him to roll over.

The sudden absence of sound roused Joseph, and like his captor had only a few nights before, he tested his bonds carefully and quietly. Unlike the Colonists, though, Ginawo had secured his prisoner well, and Joseph soon gave up the half-formed thought of freeing himself and trying to find the American army.

The sky was already lightening up to the east, and Joseph rolled onto his side to behold the sunrise. In it, he found a resurgence of hope, although he knew intellectually that nothing had changed in his circumstances. Something about the return of daylight made

it seem more likely to him that the elders would spare him, or
ransom him against other captives that the Colonials held.

His breath hung in a cloud before him in the crisp air, but
he did not mind the cold—better to experience the chill in his bones
than to be cold in his grave. Nodding to himself, he sat up and
made his way over to a tree, where he leaned back and watched the
sun climb until Ginawo and the rest of the band awoke and they
returned to their disheartened march.

The party had not been underway for long when one of the
twins gave a glad cry and called out. An answering call came from
the forest ahead, and the brother dashed back to speak in excited
tones to Ginawo. All of the Indians brightened up at the news he
bore, and the pace of the group sped up considerably.

Striding forth to meet them was a young Indian of striking
height and bearing, and as he reached the small party, they came to
a halt. The air was pregnant with emotion as the newcomer looked
from one face to the next, as though he could not believe what he
saw. Finally, he opened his arms and said just a few words in a
choked voice.

Tanarou stepped forward and embraced the young man,
smiling and replying with a few quiet words, himself. After that,
the rest of the party of Indians crowded around the tall young
warrior, while Joseph hung back and watched the obvious joy with
which they greeted their compatriot.

Gesturing at Joseph, Ginawo called out to him, "You
come at here." Joseph joined them, and Ginawo spoke at length,
obviously explaining to the newcomer how Joseph had come to be
in their company.

"Him am call Sokeheh," Ginawo said to Joseph, by way of

introduction. "Him lead at people of village." The earlier antipathy that he'd displayed toward the soldier seemed to have been eased, now that the band had been reunited with their tribe.

The Indians spent a few minutes relating to one another what had passed since they'd been separated, with not a few somber comments as they talked. As they spoke together, the band began walking again, following the young warrior as he led them slightly to one side from the direction that they had been marching.

Around noontime, they arrived in a small clearing, where the Indians had built a sturdy fire pit, around which they had set up an array of tents. The people of the village—Joseph figured them to be as many as a hundred Indians—crowded about the fire, each engaged in some task or another.

As the small band came into view, there was a universal shout of excitement and joy at the return of the lost band of warriors. Joseph could see many of the villagers shedding tears as they greeted their returned tribe mates.

The warmth of the fire was a welcome relief from the chill of the autumn day, and after his presence had been briefly explained to the group, Joseph was directed by gestures to go and sit by it. The joyful reunion continued to swirl around him, and he could not help but feel glad for Ginawo's group that they had found their way back to their tribe, despite the destruction of his own fellows that had enabled it to happen.

While he observed the Indians, he noticed that he was under close observation, himself. A trio of young children stood side-by-side, looking him over, their eyes wide with wonder. The boldest, a boy of perhaps eight years, finally walked up to Joseph and reached out to touch the soldier's corn silk-colored hair.

As quickly as his hand had darted out to touch Joseph, he pulled it back and retreated to where the other boy and the girl stood, speaking quickly to them. The girl, who Joseph thought looked to be a bit younger than her bolder companion, answered him and then laughed, pointing at Joseph.

Taking the initiative, the Colonial smiled as reassuringly as he could and pointed to himself. "Am Joseph," he said, unconsciously mimicking Ginawo's mode of expressing himself in English.

All three children shrieked with laughter, giggling to one another at his voice and words. Once they'd stopped laughing, the bold one pointed to himself and said, "Wopaku." Pointing at the other boy, he said, "Parakeh," and he gave the girl's name as "Tulaworeh."

Introductions out of the way, the three sat in a semicircle around Joseph, ignoring the celebratory mood of the adults around them to focus on the novelty of Joseph's presence.

Wopaku pointed at his eyes and then gestured at Joseph, asking him a question in the Indians' fluid-sounding and incomprehensible tongue. Joseph made a helpless gesture with his bound wrists, his palms turned upward. The boy repeated his question, more slowly and with more emphasis on some of the words.

Joseph shook his head, and said "I'm sorry, I do not know how to speak your language."

Again, the children giggled to one another, and chattered back and forth amongst themselves. Joseph did not need to understand their words to grasp that they thought him to be an utter idiot for speaking so strangely.

Another boy joined the children then, and after they'd

shared a giggling conversation, Wopaku pointed at the new arrival, saying in a very slow and exaggerated manner, "Polurahe." He then pointed at his eyes and then at Joseph again, speaking even more slowly for the idiot's benefit, Joseph thought.

Beginning to guess at the boy's meaning, Joseph pointed at his own eyes and said, "Blue. My eyes are blue."

All four children laughed uproariously at this, and Joseph felt his cheeks begin to burn.

Ginawo looked over at the sound and walked to where the children had gathered. He barked a stern command to them, and they immediately stood and, with sheepish expressions, returned to the crowd milling about the returned band.

"Childs think at laugh," he said to Joseph, his tone not quite apologetic. "Elders am circle now, come."

The fire no longer warming him at all, Joseph stood and joined Ginawo, following him to where a small group of ancient-looking Indians were gathered, sitting on logs or standing.

Ginawo gave a long speech, gesturing at Joseph frequently as he did so, and consulting Tanarou for comments at several points as he went. When he finished, he sat, and the elders quietly considered his story for a time.

Finally, one spoke up, asking a question, which Tanarou answered. The elder then turned to another man at the circle and asked him a question. Joseph could see eyebrows raised around the circle as they all considered the question the elder has posed.

The man who'd been questioned had a thoughtful look on his face for a long time, and then started to nod. He made a brief comment, and other elders began nodding thoughtfully, as well.

Ginawo stood, said a few words, and then turned to Joseph

to tell him his fate. With an odd expression on his face, Ginawo pulled out his knife, cut the soldier's bonds from his wrists and said, "You am now Skarure."

Chapter 18

Shaking his head, Ginawo asked Tanarou, "Why have the elders decided that we must adopt this pale man into our tribe? I expected them to trade him for our clan-mates who have been taken captive by the Colonial army, or to order him scalped, but to become a brother, to find a clan, and be one of us always?"

Tanarou shrugged. "The elders saw the wisdom of your first thought in this regard, Ginawo. They believe that the best way to ensure that our people can find peace is to understand these pale men, and the fastest way to do that is to make the one that we have captured into one of us, that he will tell us what we need to know in order to learn how we can make peaceful terms with the Colonials."

Ginawo scowled. "He doesn't even speak our tongue. The children were laughing at him earlier, and I cannot blame them. His speech sounds like a bear smacking fish on a rock."

Tanarou laughed and replied, "He did not have the advantage of being born among the People, but he has the good fortune to now become one of the People. He is a fit young man, strong and, in his own way, brave. He will make a fine warrior, in time. Meanwhile, he will help us to rebuild our village, once the danger of the Colonial army has departed from these lands."

He smiled wryly as he looked at where Joseph was being

taught his first words by the same group of children who had earlier been laughing at him. Tanarou had spoken with them while the soldier was still sitting in shocked silence, and asked them to help their new brother learn how to be of the People.

They'd taken up the task with good humor, after Tanarou extracted a promise from them to refrain from laughing at the man.

Wopaku asked, "Not even if he makes sounds like a gargling beaver?"

Keeping a straight face, Tanarou said, "Not even then, no. We did not laugh at you when you burned your hair the first time you learned to make fire, remember? That was much funnier than gargling beavers, you may trust me."

Wopaku had frowned at being reminded of the incident, but had asked no more questions. As Tanarou turned away, he heard Polurare ask, "Did you really set your hair on fire?" Wopaku only scowled and cuffed his playmate on the back of his head.

Now the children sat with Joseph, patiently saying words in the tongue of the People, and repeating them until he had the pronunciation at least close enough to be recognizable. Joseph still appeared dazed at the strange turn his fate had taken, but he was at least engaged with the children, and in his eyes, Tanarou saw a light that had slowly faded out during the days between the soldier's capture and the meeting of the elders.

Jiwaneh had even grudgingly attended to Joseph's wound, removing the old poultice and replacing it with a new one. The soldier had been impressed with how much her earlier physicking had reduced the pain, and when she had removed the old poultice, he was amazed to see how much the wound had healed.

There was still a deep, puckered hole in the meaty part of his upper arm and a short streak of red along the skin above it, but until they began working on it again, he had nearly forgotten about the pain. Of course, with the new poultice tied into place, he could feel it throbbing in time with his heartbeat, but as the bitter drink she again made him drink took effect, the pain faded away, as well.

Jiwaneh still directed a few angry glares at him as she prepared the bark—on a proper medicine stone, this time—saying, "If your friends had not shot a harmless old woman in the back, she could have helped me to prepare a far more certain mixture for you. The flame is still within your flesh, and it could easily roar back to life again, if we cannot defeat it."

She frowned at him, continuing, "Perhaps we will later try again to douse the flames with cold water. For the moment, let us see whether the bark in the poultice will do the work for us."

Tanarou had thanked the girl for putting aside her misplaced anger at the Colonial soldier, saying "There will be a time when your kindness to him will be repaid, I am certain of it."

A small delegation from the surviving villages of the area arrived then, including their elders, men of distinction who had been selected by the honored elder women of their villages.

Pointing out the newcomers, Tanarou said to Ginawo, "It is time for us to decide for all time what position the People will take in this war between the British and the Colonials. We clearly cannot remain neutral parties to the conflict—both sides will draw us in regardless, either by attacking us or by convincing the warriors one by one."

They had wrestled with the question on several occasions before, of course, but every time, they had been unable to come to a definitive decision. It always seemed as though there were more to ponder, more to learn, more to ask, before the elders could know their own will in this matter. Now, with the Colonial army sweeping through the land, they could defer the question no longer.

Tanarou stood and spoke first, as the light from the sky dimmed, and the fire in the middle of the circle lighted up the faces of the assembled elders. "My honored friends, I believe that we must either stay neutral, or we must tell the Colonials that we will support them."

A rustle and rising murmurs around the fire told him that his bold statement had gotten their attention, as he'd intended it to. He continued, pressing his point.

"The events of the past weeks have proven to us all that we cannot count on the British to provide us protection from the Colonial armies. We cannot hope to fight the Colonials off—they are too many. No, as my village did, our only option is to retreat to the forests, and take our chances with winter coming soon."

He sighed deeply. "My village will recover and survive, but we will do so with the help of some of our neighboring clan brothers. If all of our villages are destroyed by the Colonial armies, there will be nobody left to help those of us who have suffered this fate."

The angry mutters of the collected elders had subsided, but Tanarou knew that he had not yet convinced them. Rather than simply haranguing the conclave, he opted to sit down and hear what objections would be raised, that he might answer them.

Upetawa rose, his eyes flashing. "Are we to crouch and piss on the ground like a submissive wolf? Shall we play at being the pets of the pale men, to be driven from one alliance to another, from one treaty to another, from one land to another?"

He glared at the men around the fire, meeting the eyes of those who would look at him. "We are Haudenosaunee. We are feared for our brave warriors, and with good reason. Let us send our warriors into battle, taking the Colonial army the way that we have ever surprised large armies assembled by the pale men."

He gestured with his hands, warming to his counter-proposal now. "These armies are best suited for meeting with another army in a full meeting on their field of battle. We Haudenosaunee do not engage in battles of the sort that the pale men prefer, so their armies are not arrayed so that they can readily withstand us. We will attack like the smoke, springing up before them and striking them down before we disappear back into the forests with their scalps."

Tanarou rose again, saying, "Whether we attack as they expect or we attack as Upetawa proposes, they are too many, and our warriors too few, and their weapons too formidable. They will slaughter us and then move on to slaughter our clan-brothers, as well."

He grimaced, as though the next thought were distasteful to him, and continued, "We might be able to collect a few scalps, yes. But what use are the scalps of our enemies, if they have our lives and lands in exchange?"

He looked around at the gathering, finding expressions that ranged from anger to fear. "I know that we are proud to be part of the Haudenosaunee Confederation, and that our warriors are worthy of fear and respect. We did not gain that respect by throwing our warriors away in pointless attacks where we could never hope to prevail."

Upetawa scowled at Tanarou and replied, "We could at least make them pay a price for the harm that they have done. Look around this circle, and think of the missing voices, stilled by the pale men. What would be the counsel of those revered elders, were they still among us? Would Nitchiwake countenance lying supine, to let the pale men walk over us, or would he not tell us at least to strike a blow before dying?"

Tanarou answered, with some anger creeping into his voice now. "I watched Nitchiwake give up his life gladly to allow our village a chance to escape and live another day. He would agree with me that we ought to strive to stand apart from this battle, but once drawn in, we should not arouse the ire of those who will destroy us utterly.

"More death, more destruction, more war." Tanarou made a dismissive gesture. "I would rather that we stand with the Colonial people, but stand behind them, apart from the war as much as possible. I do not wish to see any more of our warriors sacrificed in a war that is not our own."

Upetawa frowned, saying, "If we stand apart from this war, while telling the pale men of the Colonial side that we are with them, will they not suspect our sincerity?"

Tanarou shook his head. "We will tell them that we must have time to rebuild, that our warriors are spread out in keeping us secure after the loss of their villages, that we must trade over long distances now to feed our people. They will know these things to be true, and will not demand more tribute of us than we can offer."

He smiled grimly. "They may not be as wise as our elders, but they are no fools. Even they can see when a stone will yield no water for their mouths, no matter how hard it is squeezed."

"What of the belts that the British gave to the People when we elders were youths?" Gukewaro and Tanarou had fought side-by-side during that conflict, and Tanarou was not surprised that he asked the question.

"Have the British honored their side of the covenant between us? I have seen no aid to our side, though they claimed to be bound by the chain."

He shook his head. "What I hope to accomplish is no more than just bringing the attacks against our people to an end. If it pleases the Colonials to see it as surrender, then I say let them see it that way. As for myself, I see it as preservation. We will better survive with their alliance than without."

He looked around the circle for any others who would speak against his proposal. None looked particularly excited about the idea of alliance, but the anger had been replaced with resignation on most of the elders' faces.

Tanarou nodded slowly to the group, saying, "Have you any more objections, or are we ready to agree that no better course of action is open to us?"

Upetawa snorted and said, "We have no choices. None of the options we have considered are acceptable, and yet we cannot simply wait for the wolves to tear us apart. We could scurry away like squirrels, but that's even less appealing than taking our place beside the Colonials as their pets."

The proud old warrior sighed. "Very well. Alliance it shall be."

Tanarou let out a great, gusty breath, feeling the momentous decision in every fiber of his being. "I will send a messenger to treat with the Colonial army's commander. The People will survive this conflict, and when it is over, we will examine the new world that is revealed, to shape our path at that time."

Chapter 19

"Jotepu!" The boy's call was persistent and annoying, and the newest member of the tribe groaned in reluctance as he opened his eyes.

What is it, Wopaku? The sun has not even risen yet. Can I not sleep for a while longer?"

"No, Jotepu, Ginawo would speak with you now." Wopaku withdrew, and Jotepu rose, still groaning and stretched, still not accustomed to the hard wooden platforms upon which the People customarily slept.

The months since he had been Joseph, and had known nothing of these people, seemed to be but a blur. Learning the language of the People, even though he sometimes had a hard time making himself understood, had been one of the easiest of the challenges he'd faced.

The day after he'd become a Skarure, a group of the young warriors had roughly awoken him, and, while he wondered in terror for a few moments whether his status had changed again, held him down while one of the elders brought a razor-sharp knife to his hairline.

Instead of scalping him, however, the elder instead shaved his head in the manner of the warriors of the People, leaving a strip of hair in the center of his scalp, but baring the sides to the air. It felt strange to him, and he wished fervently that Ginawo had taken a moment to warn him in advance.

When the haircut was complete, they helped him to his feet, and one of the women of the tribe presented him with a set of doe-hide leggings and a warm shirt of some woven material. His worn boots were replaced with soft, silent moccasins, and he spent the better part of a week being shown how to walk through the forest in them without making a sound.

As the children had been delivering language lessons at Tanarou's direction, and his arm had been continuing to heal, the rest of the village had been working together to rebuild on a new site. As his grasp of what was said to him slowly improved, he came to understand that the old site had been nearly exhausted already, and the memories now associated with it needed to be left to rest.

After the elders had selected a place not far from the old village, the men worked together to clear away the trees, their hatchets making short work of felling them, and their patient digging and leverage clearing away the stumps.

As the elder in charge of construction had looked on and provided detailed instruction, they had trimmed the straight trunks into logs, and piled them in a number of places about the clearing.

Within a matter of days, the skeletons of a cluster of longhouses had risen from the ground, and the women had gone to work, stripping the bark from elms, both those which they had felled to clear the village site and others brought in from the surrounding forest for the purpose. Weaving the bark tightly through the frames the men had built, the covered walls and overarching roofs, leaving openings in the crest through which smoke would escape.

With all of this underway, various members of the tribe still managed to find time to instruct Jotepu on the ways of the People.

The twins took him out to hunt and, until the River of the Dancing Waters froze over, Ginawo brought Jotepu along to spear fish out of it.

In addition to the fish and game brought home by the men, the women supplemented the tribe's diet with food they'd brought with them on their own backs when they'd fled the old village.

Jotepu had asked about the ruined crops he'd seen at the razed village site, and Ginawo told him that it had been a small fraction of the produce they'd had stored, and it had been necessary to leave it in order to support the deception that the village was in ill-repair, and not worth destroying.

He'd frowned and added, "It was my plan, but not a good plan. All was lost, and many good people killed too." The young warrior had been noticeably cool toward Jotepu for the remainder of the day, and the new adoptee had decided that it was better to simply avoid the topic of the old village's destruction as much as possible.

In the intervening months, it had become easier to communicate with the members of his new tribe, and he'd come to understand the magnitude of their loss. He knew that he'd crossed a milestone in his transition from Joseph to Jotepu when he'd found himself grieving alongside his tribe mates as Tanarou related a tale of Karowenna.

He came to feel deeply about that night staring up at the Northern Cross that it had indeed marked the last night of his life as Joseph Killeen. His life as a Colonial soldier, his childhood in Pennsylvania, his anger at the raids of the Indians against his neighbors, all seemed at times to be naught but a distant dream.

Lately, even his dreams had been in the language of the

People, and he often had to struggle to remember the word in English for something when Ginawo asked him. This morning, though, there had been no dreams to remember, and as he exited the longhouse to go and find Ginawo, he blinked in the bright sunlight, reflected from the brilliant white of the snow that had fallen the night before.

Jotepu spotted the young warrior near the central longhouse in the new village. Ginawo wore an uncharacteristic smile on his face, and Jotepu automatically smiled in reply.

"What reason is there for waking me from my slumber this morning, Ginawo?"

Ginawo clapped Jotepu on the shoulder, saying, "The time has come for your clan-choosing ceremony. Too long have you been without a proper clan marking."

Jotepu answered only with a questioning look, and Ginawo gestured at the dark tattoos across his cheek and neck. "These tell all who see me that I was born into the clan of the bear. Tanarou, too, has bear markings, and you, as well, may choose to wear them."

Ginawo gave Jotepu an appraising look and continued, "It is not often that a warrior has the chance to choose his own clan; even those who are adopted, as you were, are usually simply a part of the clan of their adoptive brothers. Since the elders themselves adopted you into the tribe, you are being given the honor of choosing for yourself."

He gestured with his head toward the central longhouse. "Come, we will go inside, and you will hear about each of the clans before you choose."

Jotepu followed Ginawo inside, blinded for a moment by

the darkness within, after the brightness of the snow outside. As his eyes adjusted, he saw that the village's elders were gathered about the fire in the center of the longhouse, looking somber, but not as threatening as he'd found them the first time he'd seen them all together.

Tanarou stood as he entered, saying, "Welcome, Jotepu. Today you will hear the tales of the clans. When you have heard the story of the clans, you will tell us which of the clans you will belong to, and you will be given the symbols of that clan to wear for all of your days, as a mark of pride and belonging."

He motioned to an open seat along the wall of the longhouse. "Sit, and we will begin."

With some trepidation, Jotepu sat where he was directed, and tried to make himself comfortable. He felt certain that to choose a clan would be fraught with the potential of offending some in the tribe, and the fact that it was a decision that he'd be committed to for the rest of his life was daunting, as well.

As he sat, the deep voice of the drums sounded from the dark far corners of the longhouse, and Taranou's voice sang out in a chant, sung to the beat of the drums. So began the tales.

Chapter 20

"In the time before even the Great Law of Peace was established, there lived a very wise young man, who was given the name Ronikonhrowanen, 'He Who Has Great Ideas.' When the People found themselves needing to divide the responsibilities of following the ceremonies required of them, he pointed out that nature divides its houses into families, without dividing the houses.

"Thus are there oceans, lakes, rivers and seas, yet all are water. Likewise, the birds are divided into eagles, robins, cardinals and crows, yet all are birds. He suggested that the People divide themselves so that they could properly share their duties, and yet remain as one People.

"The elders saw the wisdom of this idea, and he instructed the People to pay close attention to their surroundings, the animals that they noticed as they went about their business.

"The next morning, as an elder woman of the tribe was getting water from the river, she saw a deer watching her. She came back and told Ronikonhrowanen what she had seen, and he told her that she and all of her children forever would be of the Deer clan.

"Another elder woman went to gather berries to feed the tribe, and saw a bear eating the same berries some distance away. She returned and Ronikonhrowanen told her that her children would all belong now to the Bear clan.

"The next elder woman went to the lake for fish, and saw an eel looking up at her through the water. When she told Ronikonhrowanen about it, he named her the mother of the Eel clan.

"When another elder woman came back from the bog where she had been collecting plants for medicine, and told Ronikonhrowanen that a snipe had walked up to her and had shown her no fear. He told her that it was because she and her children were of the Snipe clan.

"The next day, as an elder woman got water for the morning meal, she heard a noise and looked up to see a wolf staring at her. Thus she became the mother of the Wolf clan.

"Another elder woman was looking for wood for a fire, and a beaver startled her, slapping the water with his tail. She told Ronikonhrowanen of it, and he told her that she and all her children would forever be of the Beaver clan.

"The last remaining elder woman of the tribe was looking for mussels to feed the tribe for dinner, and saw a turtle sunning itself on a rock in the middle of the lake. When she told Ronikonhrowanen about this, he said that she was to be the matriarch of the Turtle clan.

"Thus it was that our clans were formed. It has ever since been our rule that no man may marry a woman of his own clan, and that when he does marry, he lives in the longhouse of the clan of his wife's mother, and his children will be born into her clan.

"All members of a clan are brothers, regardless of which tribe they belong to within the Haudenosaunee Confederation. You may recognize the members of your clan by the markings that they wear, wherever you go.

"In our history, there have been great and wise men from every clan, and respected warriors. No clan has a claim on honor above any other, and all clans have had their share of bad men.

"In choosing, you should consider which of the clan's totem animals have given you a sign as you have lived among us, and which of them feels like it represents somehow your spirit in this world.

"Take what time you may need to consider this decision, and when you have the answer, speak the word."

Tanarou now fell silent, though the drums continued to sound. As Jotepu pondered the different clans, he remembered the deer that they had seen on the day of his capture. He could not remember even having encountered any of the other totemic animals, so after a few moments, he spoke.

"I shall be a member of the Deer clan, in honor of the deer that jumped up before us as we traveled together to this place. I have seen no bear, heard no wolf, encountered no beaver, nor any of the others."

Tanarou nodded. "So it will be. Come forth, and we will give you the mark of the deer, that all may know you as their clan-brother, for the rest of your days."

Jotepu stepped forward, and an elder he had not seen before beckoned him to lay down flat on his back, facing upward to the sky. As his head came to rest on the platform before the elder, the drums were silenced. Searching the old man's eyes as he looked up into them, Jotepu saw understanding and compassion, but also a steadiness that would admit no infirmity, despite his years.

The old man's voice sounded like gravel rolling in a barrel.

"When I give you the mark of the deer, it will hurt, Jotepu, more than anything else you have ever felt. It will be a test of your ability to tolerate pain, and will give you the strength to know that other pain will never be so bad as this."

Jotepu nodded, feeling more trepidation than before, but determined to show himself worthy.

"If you cry out, the members of the Deer clan will cry out with you. To avoid this, I offer you a leather strap to bite down upon."

Jotepu accepted the strap, placed it between his teeth, and nodded again to indicate that he was ready.

The old man bent over his face, holding an intricately-carved piece of wood, into which had been embedded the sharpened jaw of a fish. Focusing closely on the skin of Jotepu's brow, he placed the jaw against the younger man's forehead, and then began tapping it with his thumb, driving the sharp point into the skin.

Jotepu had braced himself for the initial pinprick of the tattoo, and was surprised when it did not hurt as much as he expected. Over the next few minutes, however, as the old man's tattoo tool ranged over his face, as far down as his cheek and even up into his hairline, the pain began to build, until he was biting down onto the strap.

He could feel the trickle of blood down the side of his face, and could even smell the sharp, fresh-cut iron scent of it. A rivulet ran down the edge of his brow and pooled inside his ear, the warmth of it contrasting with the cooling of the sheen on his face.

When the elder reached down and brought up a pinch of powdered charcoal, which he sprinkled over Jotepu's ravaged skin, and then pushed deeply into the puncture wounds, the younger man's eyes went wide for a moment, and then rolled upward into his head as he lost consciousness.

The old man did not slow down, but continued to work methodically and efficiently, completing the design as Jotepu passed in and out of awareness. The charcoal as it was driven under his skin burned as though his face had been lit on fire. However, with the aid of the strap, he mastered the urge to cry out, and at long last, the elder sat back, nodding in satisfaction.

"It is done, Jotepu. I welcome you to the Deer clan, and I hope that you will share in the rich history of our people. Go with Mehwaro to complete your rebirth as a Deer."

He gently pulled the strap from Jotepu's mouth and offered his hand to pull the young man up to a sitting position. The eyes of the elders upon him, Jotepu could feel their cool appraisal of him, and the approval in their expressions heartened him.

The warrior Mehwaro, whom Jotepu recognized as the one who'd brought water to Jiwaneh when she treated his arm, stepped forward. Jotepu gave him a crooked smile and said quietly, "It seems that you are always to be present when I am in agony."

Mehwaro said nothing, but smiled quickly in reply. Leading Jotepu to a freshly-dug hole in the corner of the longhouse, he turned the newly-tattooed youth and had him back into the excavation. The drums began to sound again, and Mehwaro began to chant.

"Jotepu, you are now to leave your life behind and lie in the grave that has been prepared for you. Your life without a clan is now ended; when you rise, you will rise as a Deer." As he sang, he guided Jotepu to lie on his back in the hole, which the youth found had been lined with a soft and supple deerskin.

Jotepu found it a relief to lie down again for a moment, as

his face was still an agony, and throbbed in time with the drumbeat. The cadence of the drums now increased, rising away from the speed of a calm heartbeat to the racing of the pulse one might experience after a long run, or a desperate fight.

Wrapping Jotepu in the deerskin that had lined the shallow grave, Mehwaro lifted him back to his feet and led him back to the fire in the center of the longhouse.

There, the old tattoo artist spoke over the drums, "You are now born a second time, Jotepu, born without mother and born without father, but born with a family nonetheless. Your clan-brothers everywhere will know you and will offer you their help, if ever you should require it."

Raising his hands above Jotepu, he intoned, "Likewise, you are expected to offer help to any clan-brother who claims it, so long as you shall live."

Turning back to the elders, he shouted to the crescendo of the drums, "Let us celebrate the birth of our brother Jotepu, and feast this day in his honor!" The elders answered with a long ululation, and the drums again fell silent as the throaty cries of his tribe mates echoed in Jotepu's ears.

Chapter 21

"Jotepu, do you know this plant?" Ginawo beckoned him over, gesturing at a small knob of green that had pushed its way through the melting snow of the early spring. Looking at it, Jotepu could see that the snow was actually melted away from the plant.

Jotepu shook his head, "No, I have not seen it before. What is it?"

"It is the skunk cabbage. Here, smell it." Ginawo bent and broke a leaf off of the plant. He held it beneath Jotepu's nose, laughing as the blue-eyed warrior recoiled.

Still wrinkling his nose, Jotepu replied, "I can smell why you have named it for the skunk. Can it be eaten?"

Ginawo shook his head, tossing aside the broken and reeking leaf. "No, it makes a burning in the mouth if you try. Jiwaneh might know of a use for it, but I know none. Sometimes, if the forage is very bad, and they are very hungry, deer will eat it, but I think it must burn their mouth, as well."

Jotepu nodded, saying, "I am happy to hear that it is no good for us to eat, as it also makes a burning in my nose."

Ginawo laughed for a moment, and then his expression grew serious. "Jotepu, I asked you to accompany me today not only because I wished to teach you of the skunk cabbage. I wanted you to know about this before it comes to pass."

Jotepu felt a chill, and his expression matched Ginawo's. "Please tell me what is in your thoughts, Ginawo."

The young warrior took a deep breath. "As you are aware, the Skarure agreed to be bound in an alliance with the Colonial side, in opposition to the British—and most of our clan-brothers."

"Yes, I know this." Jotepu felt deeply uneasy, as an alliance seemed to preclude the tribe continuing to hold him as a captive. However, his status as an adopted member of the tribe seemed to be considered different and separate from any questions of prisoners of war.

"As a part of that alliance, we are obliged to offer shelter and assistance to any Colonial soldiers who pass through our territory." He looked at Jotepu, taking stock of the man's appearance.

Though his hair remained shaved in the manner of the wartime Skarure, and his tattoos marked him as a tribe member, his skin was still paler than most of the members of the tribe, and his clear blue eyes marked him distinctly as not being originally of the People.

"If Colonial troops come to our village, it would be better, I think, for you to stay out of sight. If you wish to leave, we cannot stop you, naturally, but your village, your clan and your tribe would all feel deeply your loss, and the dishonor of it."

Jotepu regarded Ginawo with a look of puzzlement. "How would I return to the people of my birth, Ginawo?"

He motioned at the tattoo upon his brow. "None would look on me and see anything but a Skarure, or a Haudenosaunee. They would not believe that I felt any kinship or loyalty to the people of my birth."

After a moment's reflection, he said, almost more to himself than to his companion, "Nor am I sure that I would believe it, either."

Ginawo nodded slowly, saying, "When the People have adopted warriors from other tribes in the past, there has always been that question, both for themselves and for those around them. It is best for everyone if the issue is not raised, and so I come to you and ask you to avoid contact, if any Colonial forces shelter with us."

Jotepu nodded, looking away into the forest, contemplating the shoots of green that appeared on the saplings under the canopy of trees.

As a child, he had loved those first signs that the snow was soon to be ended, that the air would smell of earth and grass again, rather than ice and smoke. The ebb and flow of the seasons had marked his youth, and he welcomed them all the more in his current circumstances.

"I will do as you suggest, Ginawo. I think it is for the best."

"I am glad to hear it, Jotepu. It is no easy thing, being taken away from what you've known. I have met others, though, who have been able to not only find their place afterward, but who felt that it was the best thing that had ever happened to them."

Ginawo nodded respectfully to Jotepu. "You are strong in your spirit. I am sure that you will continue to find your way as one of the People. We ought to return to the village now; I do not see any sign of game today."

"Thank you, Ginawo. I appreciate your belief in me, and I feel certain that I will live up to it."

Jotepu gestured up the slope toward the village. "Lead the

way, my brother."

When they arrived at the village, Jiwaneh was waiting for Ginawo, a look of mingled fear and excitement on her face. "My time is late, Ginawo. The full moon has come and gone, and still I do not bleed as the moon would have me do."

She looked up at him, a smile playing on her lips as realization dawned in his expression. "We are going to have a child, Ginawo."

Ginawo pulled her to him and cried out, "Our child will have the best mother any could ever wish in you."

After a moment, he held her at arm's length, and said, "A child... I am to be a father." He embraced her again, and then released her, his face assuming a worried and serious expression.

"You must have no nuts. Fortunately, you have not had any since fall, so we need not worry about the child's nose being stuffy because you had too many nuts from the hickory. Have you enough warm skins, or do you need me to find some more deer? I can go further and hunt for some if you need."

Jiwaneh attempted to answer, but Ginawo continued, unabated. "You must not work any longer on the carcasses when we bring them in; leave that to other women."

He looked at her neck and hands quickly, saying, "Good, I see that you have removed your necklaces and bracelets already, to keep our child safe in birth. You must not braid your hair until after the baby is born, either, of course."

"When we observe the Ghost Dance, you must not join us, nor join in any o—"

He was silenced abruptly as she placed her fingers upon his lips, looking fiercely at him. "Do you think that I do not know all of this already? Karowenna taught me well, and Patanareh has already said that she will stay with me until the child is born, as she is not needed in her own village at this time."

She scowled at him again, adding, "I will take no rash chances with our child, but neither will I be terrified of every shadow, nor see ill omens in every cup. Patanareh will guide me and ensure that bad spirits are kept away from our child, and you need worry about nothing."

She pulled him into another embrace, then released him. "Now go, and tell the elders of our good fortune. Some cheerful news will do them good, I think. When you are done, then you may go in search of more dry wood for the fire, rather than deer for their skins. That will keep me warmer, since the weather will not be so bitter again until well after our child is born."

He nodded, not trusting himself to speech any longer, and turned to go to the central longhouse. Before he entered, he turned and said, "Be sure that when you go in through a doorway, you do not stop, but enter all the way and then come back out."

Closing her eyes and smiling indulgently, Jiwaneh waved him in through the door and turned to go back to where Patanareh waited for her.

Entering the warmth of the central longhouse, Ginawo respectfully sat and listened to the ongoing discussion while he waited for a chance to speak without interrupting.

Upetawa was reciting a litany of the depredations that had been visited upon the People during the prior winter. "The pale men brought an army through the lands of the Haudenosaunee, and razed every village they found. It was not just our village, but all villages. Skarure, Mohawk, Onondaga, Cayuga, Seneca, all burned, if the pale men found them."

He spat into the fire, warming to his subject now. "Those of the British-allied tribes who weren't captured have now fled to the northern lands, as the British have shown no interest in keeping them safe from harm here."

He leaned back, lacing his fingers over his belly. "It was wise indeed of us to have chosen to ally ourselves with the Colonials, for our own safety, but they have proven themselves to be vicious in the reprisals that they visited upon us all for the actions of a few."

Gukewaro spoke, shaking his head. "We should have allied with the Colonials before they burned our village, but now that we have done so, we should neither expect any more trouble, nor go trying to find any more trouble."

Tanarou now took notice of Ginawo's entrance and called out, "My young friend, what brings you to visit our circle of old men arguing about that which they cannot now change?"

Ginawo answered, "Honored elders, I am to have—that is, Jiwaneh is going to have our child. She has just missed her first moon's blood, she told me, and she has arranged for Patanareh to care for her."

The elders sat quietly, nodding to one another, until Gukewaro spoke up saying, "It is good to see our tribe growing further through the natural ways of childbirth, as well as through the adoption of our enemies. You have had a part in both this season, Ginawo, and your honor with the tribe grows with each feat."

Ginawo lowered his eyes, and felt the heat rushing to his face. "I have only done as I had thought that the elders would expect of me."

Tanarou added, "Ginawo, you are to be congratulated, and

we will soon have a feast to welcome your child. You have proven that you can grow the tribe; now you must feed it, too. How goes the hunt?"

As the elders continued to ask him about the mundane details of hunting in the forests, already depleted by the passage of so many men through them of late, Ginawo could not help but feel disappointed that they did not share his elation at Jiwaneh's news.

He shrugged inwardly. It was to be expected that dried-up old men would have little interest in the affairs of the young and vital, he supposed. The warriors of the village, though—they would be excited.

"I will range out to the other side of the River of the Dancing Waters," he said finally. "There, I expect to find at least some deer, if not elk. The village and my child will eat well; I will see to it, revered elders."

"Very well, Ginawo. Thank you for your news, and we will be waiting to hear details from you as you learn them."

Ginawo nodded respectfully, and then stood to leave the longhouse.

As he reached the door, Gukewaro called out, "Do not permit Jiwaneh to play with the babies of the other women, Ginawo, lest your child becomes jealous, and the other women's babies become cranky and keep us up all night with their crying."

Ginawo nodded, and exited the longhouse with a smile on his face.

Chapter 22

Grimacing, Sokeheh drank the concoction that Ginawo placed in his hands, and after he had swallowed, he twitched theatrically and complained, "This tastes even worse than when Jiwaneh makes it!"

"You know that since she carries my child, she cannot have anything to do with our preparations, Sokeheh. I used the bark of the trees she told me of to make it. Although," he added, looking into the cup with a momentary doubt showing on his face, "I do not know if she steeps it for so long as I did."

Draining the cup himself, he said, "In any event, we must be purified and ready before the sun reaches the top of the sky." He stood to one side as Sokeheh retched and vomited, bracing himself on a tree.

Wiping his mouth with the back of his hand, Sokeheh said, "Do you think we will prevail against our enemy today?"

Ginawo clapped him on the back, saying, "With you leading us? Of course we will. Besides, I have wagered much on us, so we have little choice but to win." He grimaced and turned away, leaning his hands on his knees as he vomited in turn.

Standing and steadying himself with a hand on his friend's shoulder, before launching himself between the trees, he called over his shoulder, "Now, can you beat me to the river?"

With a whoop, Sokeheh chased through the woods after

Ginawo, his longer limbs enabling him to quickly catch up and then pass his friend. Within a few paces of one another, they burst out of the forest onto the short embankment that overhung the river at this point, and jumped headlong into the rushing waters.

Sokeheh rose from the water just behind Ginawo, shouting to be heard over the river, "This is colder than I remember it being last spring, brother!"

Grinning, the shorter man answered, "No, you are just older than you were last spring, and so you feel the chill of the mountain snows more keenly this year." Ginawo ducked under his companion's playful attempt to dunk his head, and swam for shore.

Sokeheh followed, and together, the two men made their way back out of the water and returned to where their ceremonial breechclouts were hung. Tying their belts and looping the decorated cloth through, front and back, they finished dressing.

Calling ahead to Sokeheh, whose longer stride quickly put him in the lead on their way back to the village, Ginawo asked, "Is your club prepared?"

"My grandfather's club burned when the pale men came, of course, but I have made a new one. It is not as good as his—we cannot find such strong sinew in these days as they could then—but it is a good club, yes. Have you completed yours, as well?"

Ginawo nodded. "Yes, though like you, I am not so fond of it as I am the one that I lost in the fire. However, with all the deer that I have needed to hunt these past weeks in order to be sure that Jiwaneh had enough skins to keep warm and meat to eat, I have had a good selection of sinew to choose from. It is no better a club than my skill justifies, however."

Sokeheh grinned, answering, "Well, we will soon enough be ready to take the measure of your skill—and mine—against our enemy."

The two men entered the clearing where the village lay. It had been enlarged throughout the winter, and to one side stood a barren stretch of ground, around which the members of the tribe and their enemy were already gathering.

Tanarou spotted the two young men approaching and called out to them, beckoning them to his side. "It does my heart good to see you two ready to join in this battle," he said, putting his hands on the young men's shoulders.

He regarded the field before them and said, sadly, "This is not so large as the ones I remember in my boyhood. Why, once I watched over a hundred warriors on each side contend for victory. We can only come up with a couple dozen each."

He made a sour face, but then grinned. "I suppose that we should be glad for that much, though, given the circumstances. Are you ready to join your clan-brothers?"

"Yes, honored elder," Sokeheh answered, while Ginawo simply nodded. His eyes and attention were on Jiwaneh, who stood with Patanareh, behind a gaggle of excited children. She looked radiant in the warm spring sunshine, and though she did not yet show more than he could notice when they were alone, he knew that their child grew healthy and strong within her.

He called out to her in greeting, but she could not hear him over the babbling and shrieks of that surrounded her as the boys, in particular, worked themselves up into a state of high anticipation of the match to come.

Beyond Jiwaneh, Jotepu stood, a bit apart from the rest,

visibly bewildered at the spectacle unfolding before him. He met Ginawo's eyes, and the young warrior beckoned him over with a wave of his hand. Jotepu slowly walked to stand with the two warriors and the elder.

Ginawo said, "Has anyone explained to you what we are doing here today?"

Jotepu shook his head, frowning. "No, other than that you will battle against a village of the Oneida, who, I take it, are those who stand on the far side of the field even now, glaring at us and yelling insults?"

Ginawo grinned. "You are correct, Jotepu. And if I am right about our friend Sokeheh here, and his long arms, then by nightfall I will have a new beaver pelt jacket to keep Jiwaneh warm."

Jotepu looked even more confused. "You will win this as spoils of war? Someone has agreed to give it to you already, should you prevail? I do not even understand why you will go to war against the Oneida. Are they not allies, and bound to peace under the Haudenosaunee Confederation?"

Ginawo threw back his head and roared with laughter. "We do not fight today, Jotepu, but we test each other in a game of skill. When it is over, the winners will collect their wagers. This is no war, although we prepare for it as though it were, I will admit."

Jotepu stood shaking his head, trying to avoid letting his own face break into a smile. "I had wondered why the women and children did not flee at the approach of the enemy village's people."

He nodded, finally letting himself smile. "I am much less confused now. And these are to be your war clubs?" He motioned at Polurahe, his language instructor, who was running to Ginawo and Sokeheh, carrying a pair of what looked to him like stout hand-held fishnets.

Sokeheh took one of the curious objects from the boy and laughed, saying, "In a manner of speaking, Jotepu." He held it out for Jotepu to look at, but did not offer to let the blue-eyed warrior handle it.

Longer than a man's arm, it consisted of a strong sapling, decorated with fierce-looking, intricate carvings and bent over at the tip by a cord, which was fastened perhaps midway back on the length of the shaft. Between the cord and the curved shaft, a network of webbing was stretched, forming what had, at a distance, given the object the appearance of a fish net.

Sokeheh said, "You see, we string it very tightly—" he reached out to the end of the club and plucked one of the cords, which twanged, then continued, "—so that it has more power when we strike the ball."

Jotepu said, "Ball?"

"Give me that, too, Polurahe." Grinning, Polurahe produced a ball, which the tall warrior took from him and handed over to Jotepu for his examination.

It was about the size of Jotepu's closed fist, rounded and leathern, stitched tightly, and had a solid heft to it. Jotepu tossed it in his palm, and then handed it back.

With a momentarily wistful expression on his face, Jotepu said, "When I was a boy, we played a game with a ball similar to this, which one boy hurled toward the other, who would then attempt to hit it with a club of sorts, far enough that he could run a given distance before the members of the opposing team could retrieve it."

Shaking off the memory, he asked, "Is your game akin to this, then?"

Ginawo laughed, saying, "No, although we sometimes must retrieve an ill-passed ball. Your contest sounds as though it would be interesting to try sometime, as well. Perhaps you can show us how it is done? On another day, naturally."

Jotepu nodded, saying, "I would be honored to do so, yes. So what will you do with your net-clubs?"

Sokeheh said, "It is very simple. At each end of the field, you see the two trees which have been marked with paint and cloth?"

Jotepu nodded, and Sokeheh continued, "We will use our clubs to drive the ball between the trees of our enemy, and they will attempt to use theirs to drive it between ours. We do not touch the ball with our hands or our feet, just with our clubs. We will steal it from them and they from us, until one tribe or the other succeeds."

Tanarou interrupted, saying, "It is time to ready yourself for the match, Sokeheh. They apply the war paint now, and it is nearly time for the washing of the clubs."

Tanarou made a wry expression and added, "You are fortunate that you are not playing as we did when I was a young warrior. In those days, we would not merely apply war paint, but we scratched our arms and legs to prepare ourselves for the ordeal to come, so that we would not feel the pain of our injuries during the match. You have it too easy."

Ginawo smiled and said, "We still must suffer the wounds of the battle, revered elder. However, the war paint will protect us from the blows of our enemies, and we must go and receive that protection now."

Guiding Sokeheh away to where the rest of the warriors

were lining up before the elder Opetuwa as he applied the protective swathes of ochre and black to their bodies, Ginawo said to the tall warrior, "He may think that we do not battle so fiercely as he did in his youth, and yet I think that you would have beaten him, my brother."

Chapter 23

The two tribes ranged up and down the field all through the afternoon, and although Jotepu attended the action closely, he could not conceive of how the players achieved some of their feats.

The twin brothers, Itararo and Hatopeh, seemed to be able to communicate with one another using no words, passing the ball between them as they moved up and down the field, sometimes without so much as glancing to see where the other was.

Watching Sohkeheh play, he could see immediately why the warrior's extraordinary height was an advantage in the game. He could reach his club into a knot of warriors battling for control of the ball, and pluck it out of their midst, carrying it away in his net at a speed that only a few of the enemy players could match.

After watching him do this on one occasion, Jotepu had been puzzled to see the tall warrior slow to a walk just before he carried the ball between the enemy's trees at the far end of the field. The nearest warrior was a dozen paces behind him, and Sokeheh fixed him with a taunting smile as he stepped deliberately between the trees.

Jotepu was unprepared for the explosion of cheers and laughter that erupted all around him, and Tanarou leaned over after the People had quieted down somewhat to explain, "Sokeheh has shown the enemy that he can walk the ball across their line as though they were but ghosts to him. He showed them that the ball lay on his club as he entered."

Looking across to the other side of the field, Jotepu could see that the boisterous mood of the People was not shared by their enemies, many of whom sat with their arms crossed, and all of whom maintained a stony silence at the moment.

"Our enemies do not seem to appreciate his qualities," Jotepu observed, and Tanarou roared with laughter.

A few minutes later, though, the tribes' positions were reversed, with the enemy's onlookers cheering wildly while the People sat silently. One of the enemy players, a compact, lithe warrior, had performed an impossible-looking twist in the air, with the ball never leaving the net on his club, despite his gyrations.

He'd eluded the warriors who'd stood between him and the gate, twisting and turning, and despite the crescendo of hisses from the crowd around Jotepu, had passed through with the ball still upon his club.

Tanarou leaned over again, this time saying, "He does not exhibit honor by dodging our warriors. It is a disgraceful thing to see, a warrior who avoids an honest test of strength against another warrior, and instead dances away like a blue jay harassing a crow."

The elder nodded in satisfaction a few minutes later when the same enemy player was struck by a club swung at the ball in an apparent accident. Though not seriously injured, the impact of the heavy club across the warrior's chest had caused the man to pause for a long moment, staggered.

When he jumped back into the fray, he moved much more stiffly, and now suffered collisions with other players as often as seemed typical. Tanarou leaned over yet again, saying with a smile,

"Now he plays with more honor."

Jotepu smiled back, but was not sure that he understood how it demonstrated less honor to have the skill to evade avoidable contact in the course of the game. He continued to reflect on this as the game continued, eventually realizing that it was likely illustrative of the broader approach of the People to warfare—when a challenge was offered, it was considered to be dishonorable to find a way to step aside.

Indeed, this differed deeply from his prior experiences as a Colonial soldier. The Colonial officers were well-known for avoiding combat when the result would be a certain defeat for their forces, opting instead to wait for another day when the odds were more in their favor.

One soldier Jotepu had spoken with in his former life among the Colonials had been deeply upset at this practice. He'd said, "They care not for seeking revenge for our hurts while we yet feel the pain and will be the most effective for it. Nay, we must wait for the perfect opportunity—even if that perfect moment never arrives."

Remembering the soldier's words put Jotepu into a deeply reflective mood, and so he was not watching the field when Sokeheh leaped over an opposing warrior who had dropped his own club and simply rushed at the tall warrior, seeking to drive him to the ground with a flying tackle.

The shouts and jeers of the crowd around him brought Jotepu's attention back to the action of the battle before him, and so he was watching when Sokeheh continued running all the way to the other end of the field and through the enemy's trees for the seventh and final time, winning the contest.

The players streamed off the field, seemingly unaware of the mud that covered their legs, and in many cases, much of the rest of their bodies, never mind the blood that streamed down several of their faces, and welts that rose upon their backs, shoulders or legs.

Ginawo had a gash across his brow, an injury Jotepu had winced to witness take place as the warrior had run full-on into the club an opposing player had held out to try to catch the ball as it flew wildly through the air toward him.

Sokeheh, on the other hand, appeared to be completely unscathed, other than the mud he'd churned up onto his lower legs as he'd run all afternoon. Smiling hugely, he watched as Ginawo, heedless of his hurts, had gathered up the fine beaver pelt jacket from the wager stands and brought it over to drape around Jiwaneh's shoulders.

"I hope that this keeps you warm on any cold nights that may come between now and when our child is born," he said. "And I know that it will keep you warm as you bear more children for me, and give me a fine great family in the years to come."

She pulled the opulent jacket close around her and said, "I thank you, Ginawo, for this gift that you have earned by your skill and strength."

Frowning, she added, "Now, let us get your wounds dressed, lest you bleed all over me."

Chapter 24

A cicada's scream pierced the afternoon heat, and beside Ginawo, Jotepu startled slightly at the noise. Before them, the buck they had been tracking spotted the motion and leaped over a thicket, disappearing into the forest.

Ginawo stood, and put away the arrow he had already nocked, favoring Jotepu with a sour expression. "Have you never heard a cicada before today? Here, let me show you what scared you so much that you chased dinner away." He stood and examined the sunny side of a nearby tree for a long moment, before snatching something up and carrying over to where Jotepu sat still, his ears burning in shame.

His shame was not abated at all when Ginawo came back, something cupped in his hand. He thrust the hand into Jotepu's face and opened his fingers a bit, saying, "This is not the most frightening thing in these woods, my brother."

The creature Jotepu saw between Ginawo's fingers was an extraordinarily ugly insect, with great bug eyes that made it look like a grotesquely oversized horsefly. It was no larger than the first two joints of his index finger, a black body with large, lacy wings.

As Jotepu examined it, Ginawo said, "This is the cicada. It is the little brother to the blackbird, and a loud companion in the summertime."

He opened his hand, and the insect crawled up Ginawo's

finger and then launched itself into the air, flying clumsily to the trunk of a nearby tree, where it landed and instantly became almost invisible, blending in with the rough bark.

"They sing in the heat of the summer, and if food is terribly scarce, we can even eat them."

Jotepu made a face and said, "I would need to be very hungry indeed in order to eat something like that."

Ginawo laughed, saying, "Then you would do best not to startle the next deer that we hunt. Let us be back to the village, though we are empty-handed for this day. It is too hot for tending a fire to cook deer, anyway."

He turned and led the way, sweat gleaming on his back as Jotepu followed him. Though it had taken some getting used to, Jotepu had to admit that wearing no more than a breechclout in this weather had its advantages.

When they reached the clearing, Ginawo had an immediate sense that there was something amiss. He could not put his finger on it exactly, but it might have been that there were no children playing on the outskirts of the clearing, or that the fields were empty of women tending to them.

He shook off the feeling, though, as it was too warm for heavy work in the fields, and children were more likely to be down at the river keeping cool in the water than running around shrieking in the sun.

As he came into view of the village, however, one of the women spotted him and called out, "Come quickly, Ginawo! Patanareh has been asking where you could be found. She is with Jiwaneh in the birth house."

Filled instantly with terror, Ginawo sprinted away without

so much as a word to Jotepu, who made his way back into the village, his heart heavy with fear and sadness for his friend.

Entering the relative cool of the dark birth house, Ginawo heard Jiwaneh moaning as soon as he passed through the door, a low, pain-filled sound that reminded him of the cries of an animal that had been poorly shot by an arrow, and suffered in some safe place, waiting for death or recovery. The sound filled him with terror.

He rushed to her side, where Patanareh stood chanting with her eyes closed to increase her contact with the spirit world, and demanded, "What has happened?"

Without opening her eyes, Patanareh let the chant run down to a close, and then answered, "The baby is coming, too soon. Jiwaneh was carrying water for the fields, and she felt the first pains, and by the time she got back here, the water of birth had flowed from her already."

The terror Ginawo had felt at learning that Jiwaneh was in the birth house reached a new height as Patanareh said, "Come outside with me; we must talk."

Laying her hand comfortingly on Jiwaneh's brow, the old woman murmured something to her and then turned to lead Ginawo out into the sunlight.

She looked directly into his eyes and said, bluntly, "You must prepare yourself, mighty warrior, for the most difficult battle of your life. Jiwaneh fights for her life today, and for that of your child."

Ginawo nodded, feeling as though someone had poured granite into the ends of his arms and legs. Unaware now of the heat of the day, he felt his skin turn clammy and cold as he asked,

"What can I do? How can I help to save Jiwaneh?"

Patanareh shook her head, sadly. "That is what makes this such a difficult battle for you, great warrior. You can do nothing, but must only stand aside and watch your beloved fight the bad spirits that would take her, with no help from you."

Ginawo cried out, as though he were in physical pain, and dropped to his knees. Brusquely, the old midwife turned and walked back into the birth house, returning to her ailing charge, leaving him to his pain and terror.

After a long time, Ginawo rose and went to his old clan longhouse, seeking out Tanarou. The old man rose upon seeing Ginawo enter the longhouse, and clasped his friend's hands silently, his face set in an expression of concern.

Slowly, he nodded, saying, "Ginawo, I wish that there were something that I could tell you, something to make the fear go away. There is nothing that we men can do when the birth time comes, and it is worse when things do not go the right way."

Tanarou led Ginawo outside, saying, "Let us walk, my friend. We cannot do anything to help Jiwaneh but to stay away and not interfere with Patanareh's work."

Walking together into the cool forest, the two men did not speak at first, Ginawo simply taking comfort in the elder's presence and concern. Finally, as they passed through the dappled light and shadow of the noonday woods, Ginawo began to speak.

"When we were both just small children, Jiwaneh and I played together, and she used to carry around this doll that her mother had made for her out of corn husks. I teased her about it, and one day, I took it and ran away with it, and I hid it in a tree."

He smiled ruefully at Tanarou as he continued, "She was

too proud to even ask me what I'd done with her doll, but only sat and played quietly in the dirt, refusing to even speak to me. The next day, I felt so bad about taking it that I brought it back and put it into her hands."

His rueful smile transformed into a gentler smile of memory, and he said, "The next time that I saw her with the doll, she had another one beside it, and when she finally deigned to speak with me again, she informed me that she had named it Ginawo, and that it and her doll were married forever and ever."

They walked on for a while longer, and Tanarou said nothing, letting the younger man do the speaking.

"Later, when we were perhaps ten summers old, she had been running in the forest, and tripped over a root. She broke her arm as she fell, and the old woman Karowenna set the bone, splinted it and gave her strong drinks to lessen the pain and speed her healing."

Ginawo shook his head, a gentle smile still on his lips as he said, "I gave her so much grief about tripping over that root. I told her that the tree had named the root for her, and that she ought to find a track through the forest that permitted her to avoid that path."

He looked up at Tanarou, who smiled and nodded for him to continue. "In truth, she was as graceful as a heron in flight when she ran, and I was jealous of her for how fleet and nimble she was. I found out that she took my advice, though it was meant in jest, and broke a new trail through the forest—and up a cliff as tall as she was—so that she could simply avoid passing by that same tree."

Tanarou said, "She has always taken you seriously, even when you did not."

Ginawo replied, "I see that now, of course, but at the time, I thought that she was only mocking me. It wasn't very much later that my voice began to change, and I went away to stand the trials of manhood. When I came back, she was... changed, and I could not help but take notice. Perhaps it was I who had changed, but in any event, I began actively courting her interest."

He smiled broadly now. "She was terrific at anticipating my interest and deflecting it. It was fitting revenge for the many times that I teased her when we were younger, and it made me pursue her with all the more energy."

Lost in a reverie of memory now, he said, "She was so beautiful when her time of womanhood arrived, and I decided that I wanted very badly to make her my wife. She made a show of resisting me, but I knew in my heart that she had long since decided to be with me."

Grimacing, he said, "Of course, then the Colonial army came to burn our village, and when it seemed as though we might not have any more time together at all, we both knew that the time for childish games was over. And now... now I might lose all time with her. I cannot bear that thought, revered elder!"

Tanarou put his hand on his young companion's shoulder, and said nothing, just walking with him, bearing witness to his pain. Finally, Ginawo exclaimed, "I cannot take this any longer! We must return to the village, and see whether there is news of her health, and the baby's."

Silently, Tanarou nodded, and they turned back to the village. "Whatever comes to pass, Ginawo, you are strong enough to make your way through the days to come. Whether you are to be a father today or not, the path ahead of you is filled with twists and turns, and you will need that strength."

When they returned to the village, Ginawo said, "Thank you, respected elder, for your wisdom and patience, and for your guidance. I will come to you again if I need more of the same, and I will send word as soon as the outcome of Jiwaneh's battle is known."

Tanarou again clasped Ginawo's hands, saying, "You are welcome to my advice whenever you wish it, my young friend. Now, go to your wife and child." He released the young warrior's hands, and, with a look of haunted sadness coming over his face, he walked back toward his longhouse.

As the old man departed, Ginawo went immediately to the birth house and rapped gently on the doorway to gain Patanareh's attention. The old woman came outside and Ginawo took note of the sweat upon her forehead, and dampening her hair.

Without waiting for Ginawo to ask, she said, "Jiwaneh is resting now, but she has been working very hard all day. The baby is no nearer to birth, and she is tiring. I have given her a drink that will let her gather her strength for a while longer, and then her fight will begin anew."

Ginawo asked, with a note of desperation in his voice, "Is there still nothing that I can do? New herbs I can gather, no water to fetch, no food to have prepared for her?"

Patanareh shook her head. "It is always this way for fathers. You will do your part when this is over," she said, and then turned and went back inside, muttering under her breath, "...though that part might be no more than to bury her bones."

Ginawo returned to the dark confines of his own longhouse, and curled up on his sleeping platform to wait for the time of waiting to be over. Restless, though, he found that he was driven to go back outside and busy himself with mindless manual labor of stripping and straightening saplings for use as arrow shafts.

As the sun fell beneath the crowns of the trees on the edge of the clearing, bringing some relief from the heat of the day, Jiwaneh's cries again rose from the birth house, and the women of the village shook their heads and spoke quietly among themselves.

All of the women knew that Jiwaneh's time was not yet due, that the corn had only begun to ripen, and she should not have been bringing forth Ginawo's child until the first flurries of snow were in their air.

They traded stories of pregnancies gone wrong in the past, both their own and those of women they had known. While they cherished the sacred gift of the ability to bring forth new life into the world, they were fully aware that this gift brought with it the price that the process did not always end in success.

With each cycle of cries or moans that could be heard in the still, close air, someone else would remember a birth that had ended in disaster, and make a comment about it. Inevitably, the conversation finally turned to the tale of the Sky Mother.

The Sky Mother fell to earth, landing on the back of the turtle. There, she was befriended by the frog, who brought to her mud from the bottom of the sea, that she might walk in circles and spread it to form the land. Then, she had given birth to twins, and had lost her life in that process.

In her tale, her sacrifice had been redeemed by the birth of her sons, one of whom had become the Creator. The other had become the Mischief Maker, and their mother's body had fertilized the Earth. One of the women wondered aloud whether Jiwaneh's sacrifice would be redeemed, or whether she might even survive to raise her child.

The sky began to darken with the setting of the sun, and Jiwaneh's cries became less and less audible outside of the birth house. As the first stars began to glitter in the blue-black of the night, Patanareh emerged, looking grey and haggard.

She saw Ginawo, who stood frozen at her reappearance, an arrow shaft forgotten in his fingers. Slowly, she shook her head, once, side to side, and then went back into the birth house.

Ginawo's cry of anguish carried over the entire village as clearly as had Jiwaneh's cries, stilling everyone who heard it. He dropped to his knees, and then sank completely to the ground, aware only of the residual warmth of the dry earth under his cheek as he wept.

Chapter 25

Tanarou noted with approval that all of the women from the village, and even many of the warriors stood about the bier where Jiwaneh's body lay, wrapped in her treasured beaver pelt coat, then bound in a woven reed mat, which Patanareh had wrapped around her tenderly, and then closed at each end, a final service to the girl whom she could not save.

Ginawo stood beside him, his eyes dry but red, and his expression scarcely registering any identifiable emotion at all. His hair hung loose about his shoulders, unplaited still, and it was difficult for Tanarou to imagine that he had ever known the young warrior to have experienced any joy at all. Beyond him, Tanarou could see Jotepu, who looked completely bewildered at the events of the past days, and, Tanarou could tell, at a loss as to how he could offer anything like comfort to Ginawo.

As the people of the village gathered, Tanarou called out to them to ask for silence, that he might speak. When everyone present was facing him and the quiet conversations between them had ended, he began.

"Jiwaneh, beloved of Ginawo, was a strong woman, and she should have had the opportunity to have raised for him many strong children. She was gifted in the ways of healing, and she should have had the chance to become a medicine woman of renown. She was a brave and bold spirit, and she should have been granted the time to become an elder of the People, that we might have benefited from her wisdom and experience.

"Since she was denied these things, we now must go forth in her place and raise strong children, learn well the ways of our forbears, and share our wisdom. We must live up to her example, as mothers, caregivers and elders.

"Jiwaneh has now gone to the Country of the Souls, where she already enjoys the cheerful company of her son, who traveled with her, and has plenty of good meat and ample corn to fill her appetite. She is forever free of the curses of pain, bad weather and hunger, and she has everything that she has ever desired.

"It is we who are left behind who are sad; her spirit is filled with joy, and we can, perhaps, take some joy from that knowledge in the days and years to come. She will not suffer the discomfort of the heat of summer, nor the chill of winter.

"If we again suffer attack by the pale men—" he gave Jotepu an apologetic nod "—she will not again fear for her safety or that of her loved ones. If the great sickness comes to the People, she will not become ill.

"Jiwaneh, our sister, is at peace and safe in the company of our ancestors, and will remain in our memories always."

Nodding respectfully to Ginawo, Tanarou returned to the bereaved man's side and stood with the people of the village regarding her bier. Ginawo walked woodenly to stand before his fellow mourners and spoke in a flat tone of voice, devoid of any sense of life or happiness.

"Jiwaneh was my light in the darkness, and she and our child brought me more joy than I ever expected to feel. Now that they are in the Country of Souls, I will live the rest of my days looking forward only to joining them there." He stood, looking at the people gathered before him for a long time, his thoughts unreadable on his deadened face. Finally, he walked back to stand between Tanarou and Jotepu.

Jotepu caught Taranou's eye, and then looked to the bier and raised a questioning eyebrow. Tanarou, divining the blue-eye warrior's meaning, nodded ever so slightly, and Jotepu took strength from this encouragement to walk forward himself and speak.

"I knew Jiwaneh but briefly, but in that time, she treated me with kindness and skill, saving my arm from infection, and likely my life. I will miss her cheer, and how she made my brother Ginawo smile."

He stood awkwardly for a moment longer, before going back to stand with his friend. Several of the women of the village stepped forward to praise Jiwaneh's skill and beauty, with Ginawo standing like a statue carved of wood throughout the entire ceremony.

When all who wished to had spoken, Tanarou nodded to Jotepu, who, together with the twins Itararo and Hatopeh and another warrior, stepped forward and took up an end of the two belts that passed beneath Jiwaneh's corpse. As Tanarou had instructed Jotepu, they lifted her up and followed him to the grave that Ginawo had dug out of the hard, dry earth.

He had already layered the bottom of the deep cut in the earth with strips of fragrant cedar bark, and all that remained was for the four men to gently, reverently lower her into the grave on the belts on which they had carried her. Jotepu stood back now, observing the rest of the burial from Taranou's side.

Two other warriors brought in forked poles, which they set into holes at the head and foot of her grave, across which then another laid a lodge-pole. Several men then brought a large number of short lengths of saplings to lay across the lodge-pole, forming a shallow pitched roof over the grave.

Once all of the saplings were in place, they brought in another thick layer of cedar and willow bark, laying it heavily across the roof of Jiwaneh's burial vault, and then sealing her resting place with the dirt that Ginawo had excavated from her grave. When the last shovel full of dirt had been placed atop the low mound and gently pressed into place, all turned and walked back to the village.

Chapter 26

Though he could feel the warmth of the sun penetrating the side of the longhouse alongside where he lay curled up on his sleeping platform, Ginawo did not stir. Nothing he could do would make any difference at all, would bring Jiwaneh and his son back. He lay awake, cursing the very breath that passed through his nose, cursing the awareness of his heartbeat, and the awareness that Jiwaneh's heart was stilled.

Tanarou pushed aside the skin that hung at the entrance to the longhouse and walked down to where Ginawo lay. He sat down on the edge of the young warrior's sleeping platform and placed his hand on Ginawo's shoulder. For a long time, neither man said anything.

"I lost my Kolirekeh when I was your age, Ginawo, taken by the Algonquin. I know how your heart hurts, how your limbs feel as though they will not bear your weight, how your memories blind you to anything that might be before you now."

Ginawo looked up at the elder, his face still blackened with charcoal and bear grease from his night of mourning at Jiwaneh's graveside. "How can you know this pain, honored elder? I have lost not only my beloved, but also the son that she bore me. He was taken even before the clan mother could give him a name."

The young warrior shook his head angrily, tears again beginning to course down his cheeks. "You cannot know my heart, honored elder. It is not there any longer, but lies in the earth with Jiwaneh and our baby. In its place is a cold, still stone, and I will never feel anything but sorrow for all my days."

Taranou's hand did not leave Ginawo's shoulder. "At least you know where your beloved lies, my young brother. I did not even have so much comfort as that. Even now, I wake up at night wondering whether her captors have given her a good life, or if she was used as a plaything for a while and then discarded."

The old man swiped angrily at the tears now trickling down his cheeks. "I do not mean to argue over whose pain is the deeper, but you have at least the comfort, such as it is, of having a grave to keen over at night, of knowing the doom that came to your Jiwaneh."

He pursed his lips in bitter thought, and then added, "You also know that Jiwaneh's last moments were made as comfortable as Patanareh's arts could provide, that she was attended by someone who showed her all the compassion and love that was possible. Kolirekeh did not leave my life so peacefully, and likely did not leave the world in such company."

Ginawo did not reply, but only turned his face to the wall again, his back forming a rounded shape protecting himself just as the turtle. Tanarou stayed a while longer, willing the young warrior strength through the connection of his hand on the man's shoulder. Finally, he rose and walked out, surrendering for a time to his own sad memories and sorrowful suppositions.

Outside, the life of the village moved on. As Tanarou moved through the clearing to the center longhouse, to sit again with the other elders, he noted that the women were preparing for the Green Corn Festival. As in all the harvests of Taranou's life, it would be marked with a dance, a match of the ball game and games of chance, pitting the women against the men.

If Jiwaneh's death had not interfered, Ginawo would even now be out with the other warriors, hunting the bear for the feast of the Green Corn. As it was, the other hunters were out observing the traditions, though they had left Jotepu, as his skill with the bow was not yet adequate to assist with harrying and tiring the most fearsome of the prey that they hunted, and he was not judged strong enough to wield a club to help deliver the death-blows to the bear.

When three men in the uniforms of the Colonial army stepped out of the woods, then, there were few to greet them. One of the women working in the fields near where the interlopers appeared was the first to see them, and she sprang up and gave a cry of surprise before racing to the center longhouse.

There, she did not rest on tradition, but simply burst in through the doorway, crying out as she entered, "There are pale men in the village! They have returned to finish their evil work!"

Tanarou jumped upright, asking, "What tribe do they come from, do you know?"

The shaking woman replied, "I do not know. One wore a hat with a blue ribbon upon it. They are coming from the direction of the broken oak, and will be in the village by now, as they were close behind me when I came to you."

Tanarou nodded his thanks to the woman and pushed past her to go outside. When he spotted the men, his heart gave a leap of recognition. As the woman had reported, one of the men wore a hat with a blue ribbon in it, and carried himself as though he were the leader of the small party.

The elder knew that the terms of the alliance the People had agreed to required that they offer shelter and assistance to any Colonials who asked it, and he quickly decided that he would need to be able to speak with them.

He hurried to the longhouse where he had left Ginawo, to get his assistance in communicating with these men. Then, his heart sinking, he realized that the grieving warrior would be in no fit condition to perform this service. He stopped and turned back to where the Colonials stood.

Walking slowly now, with dignity, he approached the three men and stood before them. Greeting them in the language of the People, he also raised his hand to demonstrate that he held no weapon in it.

The man in the ribbonned hat asked him a question, in the harsh tongue of his people. Shrugging to convey that he did not understand, Tanarou then touched his mouth, asking in his own tongue, "Are you hungry?"

The other man shrugged and answered something incomprehensible, pointing to the north, then to the west. A small crowd had gathered now, at a distance, gawking at these strange men, and Tanarou heard Wopaku whisper to another boy, "You hear how it sounds like a gargling beaver?"

Scowling, Tanarou made a decision and turned to the boy and called out, "If it is such an amusement to you, then bring here the one who speaks their tongue the best. Tell Jotepu that he is needed."

The blue-eyed warrior hurried to Tanarou, who said, "You must speak with these men and tell them what I say, and tell me what their words mean."

Jotepu nodded and turned to the Colonials. His face then registered shock, joy and fear as he saw that their leader was Sergeant Howe. Springing forward, he embraced the surprised Colonial soldier, saying, "Sergeant, I never thought to lay eyes upon you again in this life!"

Howe stood, frozen for a long moment, while Tanarou, his eyes narrowing, looked closely at the Colonial soldier and realized with a sinking heart that he had seen the man before, in the company of his tribe's adopted young warrior.

Howe took Jotepu by the shoulders and held him at arm's length, examining the younger man at a glance. Taking in his scalp lock, tattoos, breechclout and blue eyes, the soldier said, wonderingly, "Joseph Killeen? Is that you, boy? We thought you had been murdered with the rest, when none returned from your detachment."

Jotepu shook his head. "Nay, Sergeant, I was preserved by the one who spoke some English, Ginawo. They decided to adopt me, in the manner of their people, to take the place of them that was lost in battle."

Howe looked him over again, more closely, and remarked, "You look well, other than having been marked as a savage upon your face."

Jotepu reached up to touch the raised surface of his tattoo, and said, "Aye, this marks me as a member of the Deer clan, name of Jotepu."

Tanarou spoke now. "Jotepu, I see that you know this man, and I remember seeing you with him before you were adopted into the People. Once we have concluded our business with this man, you and I must talk, to decide your path."

Taking a deep breath, the elder continued, "Tell him that he and his men are, by the terms of the Covenant Chain, welcome to take shelter in our village, that we will provide him with food and any information that he desires."

"He will want to know whether I will return with him, honored elder."

"I know that, Jotepu, and I think that we should speak of this at length before you discuss it with him. Will you grant me that favor, as a brother and an elder?"

Jotepu considered Taranou's request for a long moment, and then nodded. "I owe you and Ginawo my life. The least I can do in exchange for that gift is to speak with you before I speak with this man of what I am to do with that gift."

Turning back to Howe, Jotepu said, "Our elder, Tanarou—" he gestured at the old man "—bids me to tell you that you will, of course, receive the full hospitality of the Skarure, and that we will be happy to answer any question you might have for us."

Howe replied, "I have questions for ye, of course, Joseph. How have they treated you?"

Jotepu answered, honestly, "Like a brother, Sergeant. I have wanted for nothing, and have been given much."

"Save for your freedom," Howe retorted.

"Aye. Though they have not held me against my will, neither have I been free to go." Jotepu shrugged, and then continued, "Let us speak of this further once you have been fed and have had a chance to rest. Come, have some water and something to fill your bellies."

Howe snorted, "Now I know for certain that you are Joseph Killeen. I never did meet another soldier who was so concerned with matters of the stomach."

Jotepu smiled and turned to Tanarou, saying, "Can we give them water and perhaps some of the fresh corn cakes that I have observed the women making this morning?"

Tanarou shook his head, replying, "Not the corn cakes, Jotepu. They must be consecrated by the Dance of the Green Corn, which we have not yet begun. No, we can offer them fish from the morning catch."

"It shall be as you say, honored elder," Jotepu replied. Turning to Howe and his men, he said, "Follow me, if you would, Sergeant."

As the Colonial soldiers sat, together with Jotepu and Tanarou, the elder summoned one of the women with a gesture and gave her instructions. Within minutes, one woman had returned, bearing a skin of water and a small corn husk bag of dried meat, which the Colonials passed around amongst themselves as Jotepu acted as a translator for Tanarou and Sergeant Howe.

The two soldiers with Howe regarded Jotepu with open wonder. They were not prepared for the sight of an Indian warrior with blue eyes, a shock of blond hair falling from the center of his scalp, and a Pennsylvania back country accent on his lips, albeit with an odd overtone.

Through Jotepu, Howe asked, "Tanarou, what word have you as to the movements of the Mohawk and other tribes of this region who have allied themselves with the British?"

Jotepu translated Taranou's answer, "Many died during the winter, starved or frozen to death. My clan-brothers tell me that all who remained have fled into Canada, there to remain under the protection of the British."

The Colonial soldier nodded slowly. "How does your tribe fare?"

Tanarou pondered for a long time before giving Jotepu his answer to translate. "We survived the destruction of our village last year, with much hard work. We do not thrive, and even now we mourn the loss of one of our number."

Howe answered, "I sorrow for your losses, and I rejoice at your recovery."

Tanarou nodded in acknowledgement of Howe's diplomatic comment, and then said, "I will show you now to the longhouse where you will be accommodated during your time with us."

Rising, he led the way to the guest house, and ensured that the visitors had all that they required for the evening. Emerging from the guest house, he sought out Jotepu.

"We should speak now, my young adopted brother," he said, and the younger man nodded. He took Jotepu by the arm, guiding him to a comfortable pair of seats where they could watch the sun slip behind the trees around the village clearing.

Without preamble, Tanarou said, "I believe that you should return with these men, Jotepu."

Jotepu gasped like a man who has been caught by surprise with a fist to the gut. When he recovered his breath, he said, "I will not deny that I would like very much to return to my family of birth, but how can I turn my back on my clan-brothers and my friends among the People? For that matter, how am I to return home to a people who are not fully my own any longer? I realize that I am not yet fully Skarure, and may never be, but I am also no longer fully a pale man."

He gestured at the tattoo on his face, adding, "How am I

to represent myself as Joseph Killeen, private in the Pennsylvania Militia, when I am marked for life as Jotepu, warrior of the Deer Clan?"

Tanarou held up his hands in a gesture asking for a moment to speak, and Jotepu fell silent. "Jotepu, or Joseph—" the English word came oddly to his lips "—you have proven your ability to bend with the wind, to fit into either world when you are thrust from one to the other. When you came to us, you had no preparation, no background to ready you for that transition, and yet you were able to navigate those changes with admirable strength and resolution."

Gesturing to the south, he continued, "Returning to a home from which you came is bound to be easier than coming to one you've never inhabited before."

The young man struggled with his thoughts for a moment before answering. "Would I be able to return here, if that were my wish?"

"Your place among the People is yours always, Jotepu. I would like nothing better than to see you take your place as an elder of the tribe, bringing together the wisdom of the People and your understanding of the world of the pale men."

Jotepu thought for a long moment and then nodded slowly. "So long as this is not a matter of sending me away because I am not fit or worthy to be of the People, then I can accept your words, and will do as you suggest."

Taking a deep breath, he said, "Indeed, it is a relief to my mind that you come to me with this suggestion, as the sight of Sergeant Howe and his men has reminded me of how much I have at times yearned to see my mother and father, or to visit my home and see the fields and trees where I was raised."

Tanarou answered, "I saw that need rekindled in your eyes when you recognized your old chief among our visitors. Indeed, I suspected that you would desire to return upon any contact with the Colonials in this territory, and I have been avoiding it up to this time."

Smiling at the young man as they both stood, he added, "You are a good man, and I shall be sorry to see you go. But the turkey does not belong in a nest in the trees any more than the hawk belongs in a nest on the ground, so until you learn for yourself which you are, I will not hold you here. Go and talk to your countrymen, and learn whether they will have you travel with them."

As he walked to the guest house, Jotepu pondered whether it was better to be likened to the wily, gregarious and showy turkey, or to the noble, swift and savage hawk, and which bird better represented each of the worlds in which he had lived.

Tapping at the entranceway to the guest house, Jotepu called out, "Sergeant Howe, may I enter and have a word with you?"

"I wondered when you might show up, Joseph. Come, come, have a seat, and let us talk."

Jotepu pushed aside the skin at the entrance and gave his eyes a moment to adjust to the darkness within. He walked in then, and sat on the floor before where Howe rested on his sleeping platform.

"The elder Tanarou has suggested that I ought return with you, Sergeant, and go home to my kin."

Howe nodded, considering his words carefully before he said, "Joseph, I know not how you have been treated while you have been in captivity with these people, but I would hear you say in your own words what you wish to do. I have heard tales of other men who've been taken hostage by Indians, and who had great difficulty in returning fully to their hearth and home."

Jotepu nodded, saying seriously, "I have heard the tales, too, of men whose minds were altered forever by their experiences in the wilderness, who were driven to madness by the torture they endured at the hands of savages in the forest."

He smiled at Howe. "I assure you, Sergeant, I was subjected to no torture, and my mind is as sound as ever it was."

Howe arched an eyebrow at Jotepu, saying dryly, "Is that supposed to be a comfort to me?"

Jotepu gave the soldier a wry look, and then said, "I shall not deny that I have been changed by my time with the Skarure—the Tuscarora—and that I will after this have great difficulty with calling these people savages. They are but people, whose ways are strange to us, without a doubt, but they laugh, love and lose just as we do."

His expression more somber now, he said, "Indeed, as the elder Tanarou made mention of, my friend Ginawo—he was the one among our captives who spoke English, after a fashion, and the one who spared my life when our party was overcome—he just buried his wife and child."

Sighing deeply, he said, "I am, myself still mourning her loss. Her knowledge of physick saved my life, as well, as the wound I had suffered before I joined the expedition had grown badly infected by the time I was taken captive."

Howe frowned. "Tell me about that, Private." Jotepu outlined the events of the ill-fated expedition to Fort Sullivan, and Howe shook his head, scowling.

"That Greene never had aught but ill respect for the native peoples of these parts. I am sorry that it cost him and the rest of the men their lives, and it sounds as though it were a piece of luck that you were not killed with the rest."

"Luck, sir, and the kind intercession of Ginawo and Tanarou."

"Aye, and it sounds as if you had a hand in creating your own luck, as well. McDonahugh will be aggrieved to hear that his physicking was not sufficient to stave off infection, but I am certain that he will be both astounded and pleased to learn of your survival. If you are to come back with us, you'll see him at the encampment."

"I look forward to that, Sergeant."

He took a deep breath and asked, "Tell me how goes the war, sir? All that we here have heard of it is that the British sent a small expedition back across the frontier from Canada, but it did not avail them aught, as all of our clan brothers—those of the tribes allied with the Redcoats, that is—had already fled or died."

"Aye, and that's what my party's here to learn—we want to be sure that the work of Sullivan's command has stayed done, and the settlers in these parts will not be subject to further violation by the Indian puppets of the English."

Howe pursed his lips. "As for the rest of the war, I will not claim that it goes well. In the southern colonies, the port of Charles Town in South-Carolina Colony has fallen to the British, which has put the whole of the South at great peril, as it is most difficult to supply our forces there."

With a grim expression, he continued, "New-Jersey, where most of the militia you knew under Sullivan came from, has remained under General Washington's control, and the rumor is that we are to expect aid from the French at nearly any day now. Should that come to pass, it might help us to bring this damnable war to a happy conclusion before even the snow flies."

He shook his head. "However, that depends upon diplomacy and Congress and all those dandies in their silken stockings and powdered wigs. Naught that those of us out here in the ragged edges of the contest can do about it, one way or another."

Howe pulled out his handkerchief and battered snuffbox and blew his nose energetically. "Not much else to tell. Some suspicious nonsense floating about regarding General Arnold, something about him being reprimanded for some misdeeds while he served as the military governor at Philadelphia, but nobody's bothered to share much detail of that with us."

Jotepu nodded, a resigned expression on his face. "It does not sound as if much has changed in the war in the year since I was taken captive. I confess that I had dared to hope for better notices than these of our progress against the British."

Howe shook his head. "I do believe that Mad George will go on fighting us unless the British people tire of sending their men over here to fight against their cousins, against the right of their cousins to enjoy the same privileges that they there enjoy. If they should rise up there and demand that Parliament rein in the King, then perhaps this war will end."

He shrugged. "Short of that? I do not think that even if we should be defeated on the field of battle, the British can suppress and hold us forever. We have learned too well how to use the very vastness of these lands to our advantage. We will not be smoked out when we can but travel a little further into the frontier and array ourselves outside the reach of regiments and formations."

With a grim smile, he concluded, slapping his knee for emphasis, "So, while the war does not go particularly well, I still believe that we will win victory in the bitter end."

Jotepu nodded again. "When will you depart from this place?"

"We will be on our way in the morning, I warrant. If you will join us, then I believe that we have gathered the intelligence we needed, and we can return to our encampment immediately."

Jotepu nodded slowly, his head awhirl with emotion. "I will do so, at that, Sergeant. I must take my leave of you now, that I might make preparations for travel."

"Aye, and bid your friends among the savages—excuse me, the Indians—farewell."

"Aye, that, too."

Outside, the great arc of the Path of Souls rose into the darkening night sky, near the Bear, who as ever ran away from the spirits of the hunters who travelled the path to the Country of Souls. By this meager light, Jotepu made his way to the graveside, where Ginawo, his face freshly blackened for the night, was already standing vigil.

"My brother," Jotepu said, his voice tight with emotion. "I sorrow to tell you that I will not be here when you gather Jiwaneh's bones. I am to return to the home of my father in the morning."

The grieving warrior said nothing, but his head dropped a little further into his chest.

"I wish it were not so, Ginawo. We have been visited this day by men of the Colonial army, and one of them was a man I have traveled with before. He knew my face, and Tanarou thought it best that I go with him when he departs."

"Our revered elder is correct in this," Ginawo's soft, flat voice floated across the darkness that surrounded them. "We have been honored by your presence, brother, and I hope to see you again. If not in this world, then perhaps we will all be united some day, Jiwaneh, Karowenna, Nitchiwake, my son—" The warrior's voice broke, and he spoke no more.

Jotepu, having no words adequate to provide solace to his friend, stood and provided his presence for a long time, as the stars wheeled overhead in the heavens.

Chapter 27

In the morning, the Colonials awoke to the sound of slow drums and a song of farewell being chanted by the elders in the central longhouse. Jotepu stood before them, wearing the stout new traveling moccasins they had presented to him, and a lightweight woven tunic that hung down over his breechclout.

His head and chest were freshly-shaven, as was his face, and he was turned out in the finest fashion that his tribe mates could muster on such short notice. He held himself proudly upright before the elders, willing his eyes to remain dry. Even as he departed, he wanted to retain his honor before these people.

As the song ended, he took a shaky breath and said what he'd thought out through the sleepless night. "I arrived here as your captive, and you spared me. I joined the Deer Clan ignorant of your ways, and you taught me. I leave as a friend always, and you go with me."

Tanarou spoke, his voice somber. "It is as I told you yesterday, Jotepu. Our fires will always have a place for you, and you will always be welcomed by your clan-brothers. Go in good health, and travel in safety."

Jotepu bowed his head, and turned to leave, not trusting his voice to speak further. He pushed aside the skin covering the doorway, and emerged into the bright light of the sunrise, blinking hard.

The Colonials were yawning and stretching outside of the guest house, and one of the women of the village had brought over a skin of water and another corn-husk basket, again bearing dried meat from the summer's hunts.

Jotepu walked over to join them, and Howe grunted, "Zeb here will lend you some of his kit for the trip back. He looks to be about the same size as you."

"Nay, sir, I would wear these clothes, if that is aright by you." He grinned. "They are more comfortable than my old kit ever was, and far better suited to travel in these woods."

"Suit yourself, Joseph. If you're going to look a savage, you may as well dress that way, too. Ah, excuse me, not savage, as it were, but Indian, at least."

Jotepu nodded in acknowledgement of the sergeant's self-correction.

"Have you any further preparations to make, anything to carry with you?" Howe seemed to be surprised to see that the young man carried only a small pack slung over his arms, and just a knife belted to his hip besides.

"If the hunters return this morning with their bear for the Green Corn Festival, I should like to say my farewells to them, but they may not come back for days yet, so there's no sense in waiting especially for them."

Raising his hands to show that they were empty, he said, "As for things to carry, I have not any skill with the bow, so I've not yet made one for myself, and as I am not a warrior of the tribe, I do not have a club. I have not played round-ball, so I have no net-club, either. My clothing is my only possession of note, and I can trap and find food enough along the way that I will supplement our foodstuffs."

He looked suddenly at Howe, saying, "Speaking of the which, have we time for an honest cup of tea? I've had none for an entire year."

Howe shook his head, smiling in amazement. "Aye, we've time, and the necessaries." He called out to one of the privates, "Henry, could you start up a pot boiling and make us some tea? We'll be on our way after that."

Jotepu smiled gratefully and sat beside Howe. "To be honest, it's probably best if the hunters don't return before we depart. While I will regret missing the opportunity to farewell them, there are several among their number who bear the American militias a good deal of ill-will."

Howe grimaced briefly. "I can well imagine. 'Tis a pity that these people didn't see fit to ally themselves with us before our forces rained destruction upon their villages."

"Aye," said Jotepu. "I was not privy to those discussions, naturally, but what I have gathered in living among them, they are a proud people, and some regard their alliance with us as a shameful matter, indicative of a lack of fortitude."

He leaned back, casting his eyes about the village. "Still, I am glad that they are our allies now. They are decent folk, though they be different in their ways from how you and I were brought up."

"What will you do upon your return home, Joseph? Your term of enlistment's expired, naturally, but with your knowledge of these people, you could provide a service of distinction to the militia, whether out here at the frontier, or closer to home."

Jotepu shook his head. "I know not, Sergeant. I'd not

given much thought to my future, beyond working on my father's farm until I wed. I'll learn a trade, perhaps, or else strike out for a farm of my own."

Howe nodded. "Ponder on the knowledge you could offer this army, Joseph. In your captivity, you have learned a trade, and one of no small import along these frontiers."

Jotepu nodded thoughtfully, but said nothing. Henry handed over a cup of tea without comment, and Jotepu inhaled the steam greedily.

"I had forgotten how kindly a good cup of tea strikes the nose," he said, and slurped at it loudly.

Recoiling, he exclaimed, "And how harshly it strikes the palate!"

Howe smiled and sipped at his own cup. Henry handed Zeb a cup, and then sat down nearby. His voice nervous, he asked, "Joseph—ah, may I call you Joseph?" Jotepu nodded easy assent, slurping at the tea again and grimacing. "The tattoo on your face... did it hurt much?"

Jotepu grinned back at the young soldier. "Like the very devil had taken a hot poker to my skin, Henry. And worse yet, I dared not cry out, lest I disparage the honor of the clan. 'Twere a hard day indeed, but upon its conclusion, I gained brothers throughout this territory and beyond who will know me on sight, and would lay down their lives for me."

He shrugged. "'Tis a difficult thing to explain, though. The hurt was greater than that when I was shot—" he gestured at the deep, puckered scar on his arm "— and yet, once it had started, there came a point at which I truly did not suffer from it any further."

He shrugged again, and took a swallow of his tea. "If I

had stayed among these folk, I would likely have gained additional tattoos, to mark important occasions and status."

His mouth quirked in a wry smile. "Now, these mark me as something different from what I was before." Nodding to himself, he said, quietly, "As, indeed, I am." He stared into the bottom of his tea cup for a long while, and Henry did not venture to ask him any further questions.

Howe had listened to the conversation closely, and now sat with his own thoughts as the four men finished their tea. He kept his concerns to himself, however, and when he reached the dregs of his tea, he tossed them onto the ground and stood.

"Let us be on our way, then. I am sorry that your tribe mates will miss your farewell, though, as you say, it is probably for the best. Zeb, shift one of your sacks over to Joseph, if you don't mind, Killeen?"

Jotepu shook his head, answering, "'Tis my privilege to carry my own weight, sir." Howe nodded briskly, and once the men had re-slung their packs, he led his small, strange procession out of the village, to calls of farewell from a scattered few tribe members.

As they reached the edge of the village, Wopaku stood and called out, waving wildly, "Be safe, Gargling Beaver!" Joseph grinned and waved back, and then turned to follow the other men into the forest.

Chapter 28

The track underfoot was crisp in the morning chill as Joseph came over the rise to where he could see his house. Smoke rose from the chimney, pulled to a slant by the breeze that played with his scalp lock, as well as the short hair that had grown up along the sides of his head, and tried to force its way under his leather jacket.

His step quickened as he approached the house, and as he came around to the front, he called out, "Pa, I'm back!"

His father looked up in wonder, his expression turning to shock as he scrabbled beside himself for his flintlock. He growled, "What devilry is this, that a savage should come right to my door, and call me his father?"

Joseph stopped short, raising his hands before him. "Pa, it's me, Joseph." He gestured at his face impatiently as his father looked more closely at him, setting the gun down as he did so. "I was held by Indians, and they adopted me into their tribe... this was a part of their ceremonies."

"Joseph?" His father's voice was incredulous. "Is it really you, son? We was told..." His voice broke for a moment, and then he resumed, "We was told that you was kilt by them savages, and yer Ma and I did our grieving over you and all. It just about did her in to lose you, son. And now you're back?"

He approached Joseph, his fingers reaching out to touch the

young man's face. Running them wonderingly over raised surface of the markings there, he said, "Yer Ma will be so happy to see you... so happy... let us repair to indoors, where she's resting."

Looking at his father sharply, Joseph asked, "Is Ma aright?"

"Nay, she's had a hard time of it since you left, Joseph, and far harder since you was kilt. Though now that yer not dead, that will provide her some comfort." Joseph nodded and followed his father to the door.

He was shaken by how much older his father looked than when he had left. Joseph didn't recall him having walked with a limp, nor that his lower lip had trembled when he wasn't speaking.

As the older man reached the door, he flung it open, calling within, "Sarah! Sarah, I have such good news for you!" Turning back to motion to Joseph, he said, "Come, come on in, son."

As Joseph stepped into view, he could see his mother, rendered nearly unrecognizable by illness. Her cheeks were sunken and her hair had gone from blonde to dead white in his absence. Her eyes, though, remained lively and bright within her face, and they widened as she beheld him.

"Is that my boy? Is that Joseph?" she said, her voice reedy and thin.

He flew to kneel at her side, choking out, "It is, Ma, I'm home, and I'm safe and sound."

His mother's arms rose to embrace him shakily.

"I knew that those men were wrong. I felt it in my bones that you were still alive. Oh, my little Joseph, I am so glad that you made it home before..." She released him from her embrace and turned her head to the side as her entire frame was wracked with coughs, deep and overwhelming.

He looked back helplessly at his father, who was staring at the floor dolorously.

"Can't we do anything, Pa? Has anyone been out to physick her?"

His father nodded, as his mother's coughs trailed away and she settled back in her chair, gasping. "The Reverend Pondeen came around and looked after her, said it were consumption and there weren't naught that he could do for her, aside from that we could keep her comfortable and warm."

"Well, go and summon him hither again to look to her comfort, would you?" He turned back to his mother, and his father, his shoulders slumping, turned and went out the door, closing it softly behind him.

As his mother's breathing returned to normal, she said, "I am dying, Joseph, and there is aught to be done for it." She nodded weakly, though her eyes still roamed over his face avidly. "You look like one of those Indians, Joseph," she said, wonderingly.

"Aye, I fell in with them, was taken captive, made a member of the tribe, and then released when my old sergeant came into our village last month, a-scouting again."

"They told us that you'd been taken by the savages, but that your body had never been found. I knew that they were just wrong about you being killed, but then it went all year with no word, and I had about given up hope of seeing you again."

Another coughing fit overtook her then, and when it was over, she was too weak to speak, but reached out to hold Joseph's hand. Her grip was surprisingly strong, and he sat beside her, his eyes on hers, until her hand fell slack in his own.

He remained beside her, holding her hand in his, even when his father returned with the Reverend. Pondeen crossed himself and rushed to her side, taking her other hand up to find her pulse, weak but still there. Her husband remained by the door, wringing his hands, his face screwed up in silent misery.

Making the sign of the cross again, the priest extended his hand over Sarah's head and began speaking in Latin, and it was only then that Joseph felt tears spring to his eyes. Concluding with the familiar, "*In nomine Patris et Filii et Spiritus Sancti,*" he lowered her eyelids with his fingertips and bowed his head.

Joseph whispered, "Amen," and dropped his chin to his chest, tears rolling down his nose to splash upon the rough floorboards before him.

Chapter 29

Standing before the rough timbers of his mother's coffin, Joseph repeated after the priest, stumbling a bit over the pronunciation of the Latin. "*Requiem eternam dona ei Domine, et lux perpetua luceat ei. Requiescat in pace, Amen.*" The liturgical phrases, familiar from other wakes he had been part of in his life, provided some measure of comfort, reminding him that his mother rested now in the eternal light of God, and was, at last, at peace.

As the priest continued through the Rosary, Joseph looked around the familiar room of the house in which he'd grown up. Two of his brothers and his youngest sister had all returned home for the funeral, but word had not reached the rest in time, so the room, while crowded, was not overly close.

His father looked downright haggard, and Joseph wondered if he didn't detect a whiff of rum on the old man's breath, or perhaps seeping from his pores, even from across the room. Never one to abstain from strong drink, after his wife's death, he'd been relying on it even more than usual. His hair was combed down into a semblance of order, at least, and he'd given Joseph leave to shave his face this morning, so his appearance wasn't entirely scandalous.

Joseph was aware that his sister Bridget's gaze upon his own face was weighted with something more than just curiosity. She had turned away upon first seeing him when she'd arrived, but not quickly enough to avoid letting him see how shocked she was at the tattoos of the Deer Clan. There'd been something further there, too, perhaps even bordering on revulsion that he'd permitted himself to be so marked.

As Father Pondeen completed the rosary, though, her attention, and that of his brothers as well, turned to his mother. The family took their turns kissing the dead woman's brow, and as Joseph approached her, he was aware of the candle guttering at her head, and the faint, sickly-sweet odor of her skin. He kissed his mother goodbye, and turned away, struggling to maintain his composure and the decorum of the occasion.

Bringing forth a pair of small scissors, his sister clipped a bit of their mother's hair as a keepsake as she said her final farewells, and then stood, dry-eyed, and turned away, avoiding looking at Joseph's as she returned to her husband's side.

The family walked the priest outside, and Bridget and her husband accompanied him down the path away from the house, as the family they were staying with lived closer in to town. Joseph's brothers Searlas and Patrick were staying at the family house, but Bridget had pleaded a desire to visit with girlhood friends, and a desire to avoid crowding the small space of the old house.

The next morning was blustery and a cold rain fell in fitful showers as family and friends gathered in the graveyard. Father Pondeen sprinkled holy water over the coffin and into the open grave, intoning words that were carried away in the breeze. Joseph was gratified to see how many had borne up under the unpleasant weather to pay their respects to his mother. Some, he suspected, had come out of curiosity about his return, too, and he expected to be examined closely by many of the members of the small, close-knit community in the days to come.

The priest made the sign of the cross over the body, and then Joseph, his father and his brothers lifted the coffin and carried it to the grave, where they lowered it to rest upon the damply clumped soil. The priest dropped a spadeful of earth onto the coffin, where it fell with a hollow, mournful sound.

As the mourners each took their turn at shoveling a bit more dirt into the grave, Joseph caught the eye of his sometime sweetheart Hannah. He'd not seen her since his return, and he'd been anxious to learn how she had fared in his long absence. He was saddened and surprised to see in her eyes the same revulsion at his appearance that his sister had evinced.

As Hannah turned away from him, his expression grew even grimmer than it had already been, and in that moment, he started to understand that his home was no longer a place where he was entirely welcome.

After the burial service was over, Joseph returned with his father to their house. He sat in the kitchen, an iron poker in his hand, and slowly stirred the embers in the hearth. In the other room, he could hear his father's murmurs to himself, punctuated occasionally with a gurgling pause, as the old man raised bottle to lips again.

Joseph watched the sparks fly up from the fire as he moved the tip of the poker through it again. In the gathering darkness of the evening, they reminded him of the stars of the Path of Souls, rising into the sky.

He could see his future here laid out before him as if on a scroll. He would watch his father drink himself into the grave beside his mother's, and would struggle himself to keep up the farm, while his former neighbors looked on him with, at best, suspicion, and at worst, contempt. No girl in the village would have anything to do with him, and he would remain, to the end, alone in this world.

He pondered the alternative that Howe had offered him, and found no particular comfort in that, either. Certainly, he could offer valuable intelligences to the Colonial armies, but to what end?

Would greater knowledge of the Haudenosaunee prevent the further destruction of those proud people? Would he be able to contribute in any meaningful way to bringing the war to a conclusion, when, as Howe said, it came down to the madness of the King set in opposition to the resolve of the Colonies? What role could he play that would augur to the benefit of anyone he cared about?

As he followed that line of thought to its inescapable conclusion, his mouth tightened into a firm set of conviction. He nodded to himself as he set the poker back on its hook beside the fireplace. His path was, at last, clear.

Chapter 30

Ahead, Jotepu could see a brightening in the sunlight shining through the brilliant green spring leaves on the trees, and he started to walk more rapidly. Near the fields outside of the village, he spotted Wopaku, and gave a glad shout. It was good to be home at last.

Also in Audiobook

Many readers love the experience of turning the pages in a paper book such as the one you hold in your hands. Others enjoy hearing a skilled narrator tell them a story, bringing the words on the page to life.

Brief Candle Press has arranged to have *The Smoke* produced as a high-quality audiobook, and you can listen to a sample and learn where to purchase it in that form by scanning the QR code below with your phone, tablet, or other device, or going to the Web address shown.

Happy listening!

bit.ly/TheSmokeAudio

Historical &
Linguistic Notes

Writing Ginawo's dialog in English was challenging, because I wanted to communicate that this was a bright fellow, very articulate in his own language, with very limited exposure to English.

So, I gave him a small vocabulary, stripped away just about all grammatical elements (tenses, number and even gender), and recast that vocabulary through the lens of what I could learn of the grammar of the Tuscaroran language. The result is, hopefully, a reasonably realistic rendering of how such a person would have spoken, without descending into anything resembling disrespect or parody.

A member of the Iroquoian linguistic family, Tuscaroran is spoken by perhaps as many as a dozen individuals today. When children stop learning a language as their milk tongue, it is doomed to extinction; sadly, this is the state of Tuscaroran today.

In the globally connected world, a reduction in the number of languages spoken is inevitable—new languages spring up when people are isolated for generations, a situation that is much less likely to arise in modern society than in times past.

When a language dies, though, it takes with it a great deal of information about the worldview and culture of its speakers, which makes it more difficult to understand them and to relate to our own lives. The Tuscarora, like many Native American tribes, are engaged in an ongoing attempt to consciously revive their tongue, but history records only one instance in which such an effort succeeded, and that, imperfectly—the restoration of Hebrew as the language of Israel.

In the absence of so much of their living tradition, I have drawn on a number of sources to reconstruct what I could of the Tuscaroran lifestyle at the time of the American Revolution, but much is lost to the ongoing encroachments of time and the tragically short life spans we human beings are subject to.

I am indebted to the observers of the Tuscaroran and the broader Iroquois cultures who recorded with remarkable detail traditions and ceremonies they saw in the 18th century, and to those among these cultures who have more recently taken the time to document for the world what their animating beliefs and motivations were.

The sweep of the American army through the Iroquois territory took place very much as I've depicted it, in retribution for Iroquois attacks at the urging of their British allies on American frontier farmsteads and villages. The Iroquois Confederation, the structure of which informed the Articles of Confederation—the first Constitution of the United States—was sundered by the alliance with the Americans of the Oneida. Under the threat of destruction by the American army, the Tuscarora also allied themselves with the Colonies, which further split the Iroquois.

As I described them, the ties of clan brotherhood extended across tribal lines to bind the Confederation together. The split within the Confederation resulted in a level of civil war between the tribes, and even between bands within the tribes, that was every bit as wrenching as any civil war is, with ties of clan, family and friendship being torn apart by political and military forces beyond the control of the individuals involved.

It is, indeed, one of the sad ironies of history that not only did the birth of the American nation contribute to the dissolution of this Indian nation, but worse, that it is largely forgotten. I have sought to redress this insult by respectfully, and as accurately as I could, telling this story as one of my small tales from this time of global changes.

For those readers who like to turn to the last page to see how the book ends, a huge spoiler: the American Revolution succeeded, and the British were forced to abandon all but their Canadian holdings in North America. One of the many stories of how that came to pass, however, occupy the pages between this and the front cover of this book. Enjoy!

Acknowledgements

A ny book with historical content stands on the shoulders of the countless researchers, both professional and amateur, who give the author a basis upon which to try to invoke the strange and foreign country that is the past.

A novel such as this one that attempts to give its readers a sense of not only a time long past, but of a culture that is all but lost, must rely more than usual on the good work of ethnographers, historians, linguists, researchers into the material goods of the culture, and many others.

In this effort, I was particularly aided by the ongoing efforts of the Tuscarora Tribe and the Haudenosaunee Confederation to preserve the evidence of their past, with special attention to their lore and knowledge of their roots.

I must again also acknowledge the amazing resources placed at our fingertips by the archives put online by Google in their ongoing efforts to digitize and thus preserve and make accessible the many rich resources created by writers whose work has become part of the public domain.

Finally, the incredible friendship and community offered by the many writers, publishers, and booksellers with whom I have become friends since beginning this odyssey has been a tremendous source of encouragement and strength.

Thank You

I deeply appreciate you spending the past couple of hundred pages with the characters and events of a world long past, yet hopefully relevant today.

If you enjoyed this book, I'd deeply appreciate a kind review on your favorite bookseller's Web site or social media outlet. Word of mouth is the best way to make our authors successful, so that we can bring you even more high-quality stories of bygone times.

I'd love to hear directly from you, too - feel free to reach out to me via my Facebook page, Twitter feed or Web site, and let me know what you liked, and what you would like me to work on more.

Again, thank you for reading, for telling your friends about this book, for giving it as a gift or dropping off a copy in your favorite classroom or library. With your support and encouragement, we'll find even more times and places to explore together.

http://larsdhhedbor.com
http://facebook.com/LarsDHHedbor
@LarsDHHedbor on Twitter

Enjoy a preview of the next book in the
Tales From a Revolution series:

The Declaration

Noting the color of the leaves, Justin Harris whispered reassurance to his horse as the young mare picked her way down a rocky slope. It certainly was a gorgeous autumn day, and he was eager to return to his home and family. As he began to see familiar landmarks along the road, he felt the natural tension between his shoulders start to relax.

The Cherokee had been relatively peaceful for the past few years, but the French had certainly been stirring up trouble all up and down the seaboard, supplying arms and rum to the Indians in an effort to disrupt trade and settlement in the English Colonies. Any time that he traveled beyond the settled region around his home, Justin felt that old tension between his shoulder blades build up, as though expecting the sharpened head of an arrow to bite in at any moment.

Now, though, with the late afternoon sun slanting through the trees and the trilling of the songbirds he knew so well ringing in his ears, he could relax. As he came to the bottom of the hardscrabble slope, he could see the fresh marks of other travelers on this road. Horse droppings that looked to be from only this morning made him wonder who was traveling ahead of him, and regret that he had not met his fellow traveler on the road.

Some company other than the mare would have been a welcome break from the monotony and tension of riding from

Charles Town. It was only three days' riding, four in foul weather, but one was safer in a group. The smell of fresh-fallen leaves warm in his nostrils, though, Justin could not hold on to his regret for long. He always relished the anticipation of the last few miles to home, and was, upon reflection, just as glad to enjoy them in solitude.

He wondered how the children were faring as malarial months set in. Every fall was a new terror for his young wife, as she worried over each shiver that the children suffered. Though their farm was somewhat up out of the bottom land where the fevers often seemed to reside, in a bad year, the pestilential fever would sweep out over the land, touching nearly every home from Charles Town to the Upcountry.

While his small farm could not yet justify a slave to help, Justin hoped to be able to afford the investment within only a few more years. The land was rich and fertile, and he was glad that the small field of tobacco he'd harvested last month had been so productive. It was a lot of work to take on without help, but the oldest boy would be big enough to at least guide the turkeys through the fields next summer, where they would feast on pests in the leaves.

His cousin outside of Charles Town had hinted at the possibility of the loan of a buck negro, but Justin had demurred for the time being, being unwilling to be beholden to his wealthy relations so soon after breaking off to establish his own fortune. Jeremiah had called the slave in from the fields for Justin's inspection.

"He's a fine, strong one, that Terrance," Jeremiah had said, laughter in his voice, and his hands laying across his expansive belly. "Turn 'round for my cousin Justin, Terrance," he called out to the young man, whose skin was as black as night.

"Bred that boy right here on the plantation, Justin. His mam was just off the boat from Guinea, but his pap is an old fellow who's worked for Harrises near his whole life. Mam didn't make it through the fevers a few years ago, but Terrance here, he didn't mind leaving the house when he got big enough for the fields. Didn't care for having my silly wife prayin' over him all the time."

Jeremiah raised his voice to call out to the black man. "That'll be all, Terrance. Now get back to the fields—you're behind on your work now." He gave a hearty laugh and dug Justin in the ribs. "Gotta keep them negroes hopping, you know? Doesn't do to have a blackbird sitting around, tryin' to think up ways to get themselves into trouble." Terrance silently turned and walked back to the fields, his stride long, but merely efficient, not overtly prideful.

Justin grinned at the memory, quite sure that Terrance wouldn't have been able to make much trouble anyhow. He judged himself to be good at taking the measure of a negro on sight, and Terrance did not strike him as being one to worry about. Those raised on the plantation rarely were, even if their dams were fresh from Africa.

Thinking about it, he could see how having Terrance on the farm could make it possible to plant a more ambitious tobacco crop the next spring. Have to get some more land cleared, of course, but that could keep even a strong young buck busy for months. He decided that he'd ask Elizabeth whether she was comfortable with a negro on the farm, and if she agreed, he'd swallow his pride and write to Jeremiah.

After all, if the point of establishing his own homestead was to reach the point of being independent of the Charles Town

Harrises' wealth, how better to achieve that than by bringing in a bigger tobacco crop next fall? Of course, making the shift from indigo planting to tobacco would be challenging for the negro, but nothing that an occasional touch of the whip couldn't help with.

He caught the first whiff of fragrant smoke from the cooking fire from his neighbor's place, and sat up straighter on his mare. Digging his heels in slightly, he urged her to speed up a bit, but she needed no encouragement. Her own eagerness to return to the comfort of her familiar paddock was incentive enough for her to pick up her feet and walk more smartly.

Rounding the corner on the road as it wrapped around the hill behind his farm, he could see his simple home. One day, he hoped, he'd give Elizabeth a proper plantation home, but for the moment, she didn't seem to mind it, and the children were happy with it. As he rode down the slope to the house, Timothy spotted him and started running toward him, shouting, "Papa! Papa!"

Elizabeth, hearing his excitement, emerged from the house, her face shining with her exertions in the kitchen. Justin rode up to her and swung out of his saddle, taking her into his arms for a long embrace. His son threw himself onto one of Justin's legs and wrapped his arms around it tightly, beside himself at the joy of seeing his father again. His baby daughter came to the doorway, where she solemnly regarded him, thumb stuck into her mouth. Her enormous dark eyes were like pools of ink, and after a moment, she turned and toddled back into the house.

"I am so glad to see you, Justin," Elizabeth murmured into his shoulder. "Old Thomas did come by every day, as you asked him to, and made sure that everything was taken care of around the farm, but I worry whenever you're traveling."

"I know, Elizabeth. It really is pretty safe these days, though. And I'm glad I went. Jeremiah's really becoming quite the figure in Charles Town. He also had an interesting offer for me." Justin outlined his thoughts on bringing Terrance to the farm, pointing out the advantages of being able to expand their tobacco crop sooner than he'd expected.

"I won't do it, though, if you don't like the idea of a negro on the farm, Elizabeth."

She considered for a moment and then said, "No, I don't think it will trouble me. I worry about what the children will make of it, but I know that it's important for us to be able to improve our situation here."

Justin embraced his wife again. "I knew you'd understand, dear. I'll write to Jeremiah and work out the details." He whirled around, looking at the land around his home. "I think we'll clear that section over there for the planting, and that area past there for the growing season."

"I'll be right inside—I am famished from the ride, but I want to check on the tobacco before I come in, all right?"

"Certainly, dearest. I have a good chicken stew started, and I've just got to make some biscuits. It should all be ready before sundown."

He kissed her on the side of her head. "That sounds wonderful, dear. I won't be long."

Stretching his legs as he walked, Justin strode to the small structure where the tobacco hung, drying. The rich scent of the leaves, now faded from brilliant green to a deep tawny shade, filled his whole head with its heady odor—and the thought of the earnings they would bring. He'd have to hitch up the wagon and bring them in to the government house in just a few more weeks.

The soft weight of the leaves rustled slightly as he ran his hands over them gently. It had been a good crop, with nearly perfect weather, particularly at harvest time. A long summer of careful attention had yielded nearly as perfect a result as he could have hoped for.

He reflected that he might even be able to triple his crop next year, if Terrance were industrious enough. He'd have to get a letter off to his cousin with the next post rider, though, if he were to have enough time to clear the land.

Turning to look back out over the hollow where his house nestled, Justin sighed contentedly. Everything was going to work out well, he just knew it.

Look for **The Declaration: Tales From a Revolution - South-Carolina** *at your favorite booksellers.*

Made in the USA
Las Vegas, NV
17 June 2023

73573296R00121